JOHN CREASEY

THE TOFF
AT BUTLIN'S

HODDER AND STOUGHTON

Except for Mr. W. E. Butlin, who amiably consented to appear briefly in these pages, and "Colonel Wickford White", whom some will think they recognize, the characters in this book are entirely imaginary and have no relation to any living person, although the author confesses that he finds this hard to believe about the character named Rollison.

The author is most warmly grateful to Mr. Butlin and so many of his staff for their help and cheerful guidance.

FIRST PUBLISHED JANUARY 1954
SECOND IMPRESSION   MAY 1954
THIS EDITION   1957

Printed and Bound in Great Britain for
Hodder & Stoughton Ltd., London, by
Richard Clay and Company, Ltd.,
Bungay, Suffolk

CONTENTS

The Toff stayed at Middle Camp. The horizontal lines in the camps represent 'chalet lines'—paths and lawns between long rows of chalets.

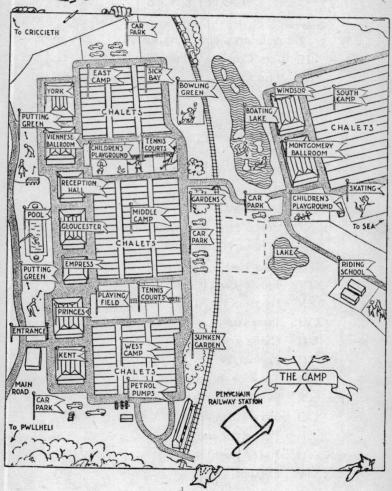

To CRICCIETH

CAR PARK

EAST CAMP

SICK BAY

BOWLING GREEN

CHALETS

YORK

PUTTING GREEN

VIENNESE BALLROOM

CHILDREN'S PLAYGROUND

TENNIS COURTS

RECEPTION HALL

POOL

MIDDLE CAMP

GLOUCESTER

CHALETS

EMPRESS

PUTTING GREEN

PLAYING FIELD

TENNIS COURTS

PRINCES

ENTRANCE

KENT

WEST CAMP

CHALETS

MAIN ROAD

CAR PARK

PETROL PUMPS

SUNKEN GARDEN

To PWLLHELI

PENYCHAIN RAILWAY STATION

GARDENS

CAR PARK

CAR PARK

LAKE

BOATING LAKE

WINDSOR

SOUTH CAMP

CHALETS

MONTGOMERY BALLROOM

SKATING

CHILDREN'S PLAYGROUND

To SEA

RIDING SCHOOL

THE CAMP

CHAPTER I

A LETTER FOR ROLLISON

"Isn't she lovely?" marvelled Richard Rollison, holding the pamphlet at arm's length. "Such poise. Such colouring. Such beauty. Look at those eyes. If I thought there were half a chance of finding a girl like it at Billy Butlin's, I'd spend a holiday there myself."

His man, Jolly, shuddered. It was a delicate, one might almost say a refined, shudder. It was accompanied by an expression not so much of horror as of hurt, and mingled with it was a little incredulity and a tincture of dismay.

Jolly had exactly the right kind of face with which to register such emotions. It was pale, lined, sad; in repose, his brown eyes had the intent look of a dog's who did not know what ridiculous impulse would take his master next. Beneath his chin, Jolly's skin was baggy; at his eyes there were dark shadows. He dressed in a black coat and striped grey trousers, and wore a winged collar and a funereal cravat. He was very much the gentleman's gentleman; and in solemn moments Rollison, the Honourable Richard Rollison, would be almost lachrymose about this, for it was so evident that gentlemen's gentlemen were a dying race.

"Gorgeous," Rollison added, not at all tearful on that warm afternoon in July.

The weather made the grey roofs and grey walls of the house opposite look almost beautiful; the patch of blue sky, visible if one craned one's neck, suggested that this might not be London, England, but some heavenly spot on the Mediterranean or the Pacific, where travel agents said the sky was always blue and the sun always shone and there was no such thing as rain except during the night.

"Isn't she?" added Rollison earnestly, and glanced up from the pink-faced, golden-limbed damsel in an abbreviated swim-suit who ornamented the front of the pamphlet.

7

He became reproachful. "Jolly, I don't think you are even looking at her."

"No, sir," said Jolly. "I——"

"Don't tell me that you disapprove, I couldn't stand it. You're too old to reform your ways. Slim and beautiful girls have always fascinated you."

"Is there anything of *importance* in the post, sir?" asked Jolly, positively on the point of exasperation.

Rollison, sitting at his large desk, with his back to a wall which looked as if it belonged to a theatrical costumier's shop, because of the variety of objects hanging on or sticking to it, shook his head.

Those who did not know him were always quick to admit that he was a remarkably handsome man. True, there were some who said that he was not so young as he had been, and it is true that *anno domini* had laid a courteous hand upon him. Here and there in his dark, wavy hair there was a tell-tale thread of grey. At the corners of his eyes and the corners of his lips were tiny lines, which grew deeper and sharper whenever he smiled. But these things were simply the evidence of maturity, mellowing him graciously. Those who knew him well at this time agreed that he was in his prime, and that he looked not a day older than he had ten years before.

Despite the tiny crows'-feet, his grey eyes often held the familiar and famous steely glint, yet could glow with laughter or burn as with fire, could stab with hostility or smile with friendliness. They were remarkable eyes, which had frightened the life out of some and the wits out of many, yet encouraged others—men without hope—to recover faith in human nature.

His mouth remained a mobile thing, capable of suggesting the whole gamut of emotions. Emotional people, teenage girls especially, had been known to hold their breath in the hope that he would smile. He had a following worthy of a film star, which was not his fault and actively distressed him.

His lean body had no superfluous flesh; all his seventy-three inches, his breadth of shoulder, his long legs, and long, muscular arms, were made for ease of movement. He was a graceful, handsome, mellow, and remarkable man of varied and astonishing gifts.

The world knew him as the Toff.

The Toff, of course, had won his spurs over the years as an Enemy of Crime. He had been called many and wondrous things, only a few of which can be repeated here, and of these the least extravagant are the Modern Robin Hood, the Gay Adventurer, and—used with much justification—the Scarlet Pimpernel of the Atomic Age.

An American once summed it up succinctly.

"Sure, I understand," he said. "The guy's a private eye."

Once upon a time, then being wealthy, Rollison had been able to investigate crime for the sake of it, not needing to earn more money. Times had changed. Poverty had threatened him, and now he used his many talents so as to earn his living. He had found this difficult, at first, and might never have managed it but for Jolly. Jolly was the Toff's valet, Man Friday, butler, secretary, amanuensis, confidant, and legman—and also his Business Manager.

Naturally, Jolly was anxious to turn Rollison's wayward eye from contemplation of a beauteous damsel depicted upon an advertisement for Butlin's Holiday Camps to letters of importance. Jolly was always looking for business.

Rollison spent thirty seconds sifting through letters.

"Nothing from millionaires wanting our services," he said. "We've seven bills, that means it's early in the month, doesn't it?"

"The fourth of July, sir."

"I shall mourn America, you attend to the bills," said Rollison sadly, and collected these and handed them to Jolly with a flourish. "We also have four appeals for help for some deserving causes, perhaps a couple of guineas each?" That was almost pleading.

Jolly took these letters of appeal firmly.

"We have *not* the funds with which to contribute to new charities, sir, your present list is already far too long."

"Pity," sighed Rollison. "Oh, well. Lord and Lady Mol-
livery will be calling tomorrow afternoon."

"Yes, sir."

"There's a letter from the Ansons, in Cape Town," Rollison went on. "They lost their dog and wonder if we'd
care to go and look for it. A joke. And that's the lot."

Jolly leaned forward, to make sure.

On the desk were other pamphlets which had been in-
cluded in the large envelope from Butlin's Holiday Camps.
Strangely enough, each appeared to have a picture of a
beautiful girl on it; sometimes with young men, sometimes
with children, and sometimes with mountains in the background. In all there were seven pieces of gaily coloured
literature. Beneath one lurked the corner of an envelope.

"Have you read this, sir?"

Jolly touched the envelope cautiously, almost disdain-
fully, as if it might soil his fingers; but he touched it. It was
sealed, and addressed by typewriter to :

The Hon. Richard Rollison, C.B.E., M.C., F.C.,
B.E.M., Croix de Guerre,
22g, Gresham Terrace,
London,
W.1.

Jolly's expression relaxed.

"What's softening you?" asked Rollison, and took the envelope. He grinned at the string of letters. "I wonder where
they raked it all up?" He picked up a paper-knife (which
had once been plunged into the heart of an unpleasant
character by an even more unpleasant character whom Rollison had helped on his journey to the gallows) and slit the
envelope.

He drew out a letter.

Across the top, waves of grey were superimposed upon
white paper. In the centre of this was the one word, in red
script : *Butlin's*. Beneath this was a tiny "*Ltd.*". The address, centred beneath the name in black, was Oxford Street,

London, W.1—hardly a stone's throw from Gresham Terrace.

The letter was brief :

> Dear Mr. Rollison,
>
>   The undersigned would be grateful if you could call to see him in the course of the next day or two. It would be an advantage if you could telephone when you are coming, but the undersigned will see you at any convenient time to your good self.
>
> Yours very truly,
Wickford White.

Silently, Rollison handed this to Jolly.

Jolly read.

"I am told," said Rollison, in an envious voice, "that this organization is large, powerful, and wealthy. In view of the state of our bank balance, I think we shall have to overcome your reluctance and your disapproval and see Mr. Undersigned, don't you ?"

"Mr. White, sir."

"Oh, yes."

"No doubt it would be wise to find out what he desires to discuss with you," conceded Jolly, choosing his words with finicky precision, "but I think I may say that our bank balance is not yet in such a parlous position that you need to accept *any* suggestion which might be made."

"Such as ?"

"I am told that this—ah—organization has a remarkable flair for publicity," said Jolly sententiously, "and I should hesitate very much before allowing our name to be used in such a connection. I would employ the utmost caution, sir—in fact, if I were to telephone Mr. White——"

"No," interpolated Rollison. "I wouldn't trust you to, Jolly. You'd probably make him feel as if he were a nasty smell. Open your eyes, man. There could be a fortune in this."

"I very much doubt it, sir."

"But then, we don't really need a fortune, do we?" asked

Rollison brightly. "Our bank balance isn't in such a mess after all. Give me those charity appeals."

"But, sir——" Jolly drew back, startled.

"I shall send two guineas to each," declared Rollison, "first because I'd like to, second so as to teach you not to mislead me on matters of High Finance." He grabbed the appeals. "Now get me the great Undersigned."

He began to write cheques while Jolly, as near glowering as Jolly could, and with an air of such long suffering, that had Rollison noticed he must surely have relented, lifted the telephone.

It took several minutes to be connected with Mr. Wickford White. Jolly leaned from one side to the other, breathing deeply; he even began to mouth words. Rollison signed the fourth cheque, lit a cigarette, and studied the letter.

A small chiming clock on the desk struck eleven. It was a remarkable little clock, of hand-beaten silver, and there was none other like it in the world. Worked on the cuckoo-clock principle, a tiny opening appeared in the bottom of it when the mechanism was set; but instead of a cuckoo, a tiny pistol and a lethal bullet appeared. A Frenchman who had since lost his head on the guillotine had presented it to Rollison—forgetting, for some mysterious reason, to explain the mechanism. A scar remained on Rollison's shoulder.

Rollison leaned back in his comfortable swivel chair, and smiled at Jolly, who stared at the opposite wall rather like a soldier on parade.

At last : "*Is* that Mr. Wickford White——"

"Colonel Wickford White," breathed Rollison, and tapped a corner of the letter-heading, whereon was a list of directors.

"Mr. Richard Rollison would like a word with you," Jolly said, in a voice which must have sounded as if it had been acquired in the Arctic wastes. "*One* moment, please."

He handed Rollison the telephone.

"Thanks," said Rollison, and made himself sound amiable. "Colonel White?"

"Very good of you to call me," said the Colonel, with

great warmth. "I do appreciate it, very much indeed. I hope you can spare me half an hour some time today, or better still"—he spoke as if he were suddenly inspired—"have lunch with me. Can you?"

"Nice of you," murmured Rollison. "If you could give me some idea of what it's about——"

"Much rather see you," boomed the Colonel. "Talk it over much better that way. I assure you I won't waste your time, and you're just the right man for the job. It's Mr. Butlin's own idea, and I couldn't agree with him more. *Do* have lunch with me. At the *Gondoliers,* in Nickle Street— but perhaps I could pick you up somewhere."

In that moment Rollison decided. It was partly because the breezy, bounding voice of Colonel Wickford White intrigued him; the voice which seemed to tell of a most refreshing vitality. It was partly because he had heard much, in a casual way, about the fabulous Holiday Camp organization, and that also intrigued him. It was partly because his Business Manager had trained him to be ready to seize any opportunity to earn a large fee; or any kind of fee.

"Nice of you," he repeated, "I will. You couldn't bring the girl along with you, could you?"

Jolly raised his hands, horrified.

The Colonel sound boisterously startled.

"Eh? What's that? Who?"

"The Cover Girl. You must know. The luscious bit on the cover of the pamphlet, whom you forgot to put on the letter-heading. Don't say she isn't *real*?"

Before he had finished, White was chuckling; which suggested that he had a quick mind and a reasonable sense of humour.

"Oh, she's real all right," he said. "If we get along as well as I hope we shall, I'll soon introduce her to you." He chuckled again, uproariously. "Shall we say one o'clock, at the *Gondoliers*?"

CHAPTER II

THE COLONEL'S PROBLEM

THE *Gondoliers* was comparatively new and extremely popular among those who appreciated perfect Italian cooking, which meant exquisite food, the best wine that the valleys of Italy and of France could produce, service second to none, and comfort and a sense of being truly welcome. Rollison knew it well. He was known by the head waiter, the wine waiter, the doorman, the lesser waiters, and—even more noteworthy—he was known by Signor Giuliani, who owned the restaurant.

Nickle Street was narrow; it was almost inaccessible. Touring Americans likened the district to Greenwich Village on a postage stamp, but it was not quite so small as that. The approaching streets were narrow, but a car could move along them—although at some spots it was necessary for two wheels to mount the shallow pavement. Nowhere could cars pass one another.

Rollison, who had walked, turned into Nickle Street at five minutes to one. It would have been hard to find a more drab prospect. Here were little houses, some turned into shops, practically all in need of a coat of paint; most, in fact, needed two or three coats. Yet there was a something which the rest of London could not boast, unless one regarded Soho as being in London. Soho was on a much larger scale than this, however. But a grocer's shop stood at the corner, boasting on its fascia board the name of Pirandello, and displaying in its window all the strange jars and wicker baskets and tins with exotic labels which one might find in Milan or Genoa or Rome. Hanging in the window were bottles (probably empty) of Chianti in their raffia holders. In odd corners were mysterious-looking cheeses, strange beans and berries in little bottles, salami, and, of course, spaghetti and ravioli ready for cooking.

It was called by some by a romantic name : Little Italy.

A large London policeman filled the pavement which led towards the *Gondoliers*. He saw Rollison, and frowned, as if in an effort of memory. As they drew level, he beamed and said triumphantly :

"Good morning, Mr. Rollison !"

"Hallo, Hubb," said Rollison brightly, "keeping all right ?"

They stopped, and P.C. Hubb—his name *was* Hubb—looked at Rollison as an incredulous explorer of the oceans might look when coming face to face with a coelacanth or any other fishy form of missing link.

"V-v-very well, sir, thank you," he said in a bewildered voice. It was evident that he wanted to ask how Rollison came to remember his name, for they had met only twice—first when making an arrest together, next when in court to give evidence—three years ago. Before then, Hubb—like many people—had heard of Rollison and been familiar with his photograph; but Rollison had not known of the existence of P.C. Hubb.

"That's fine," said Rollison, amiably. "Did you manage to get that holiday in the South of France ?"

Two minutes later, having learned not only that Hubb had taken his wife to the Riviera for a dream-like two weeks, but much of what both Hubb and his wife had thought of it, Rollison went on.

Hubb so marvelled that he passed three cars parked in illegal places without noticing.

Rollison reached the *Gondoliers*.

It looked small. It had one window, with net curtains which hid everything from sight. The door, painted bright red, was closed. The only indication that it was a restaurant was the knife and fork, painted on the window immediately beneath a gondolier on an imaginary canal.

The doorman, wearing a hat which might have come from Venice, was delighted to welcome Rollison in unmistakable Cockney.

The door opened—and the world changed. Here was a

kind of luxury land, a place of warmth and soft lighting and
gentle colours, waiters immaculate in black and white, a tiny,
cocktail bar with subdued lighting and many bottles and
one of the prettiest girls in London as barmaid. A little way
ahead of Rollison were tables with people sitting at them,
and soft-footed men who hurried yet did not appear to move
fast; and there was a gentle hum of conversation and, on
each wall, a vividly painted Venice canal scene.

A short, dark-haired, sleek man came up, and greeted
Rollison like an old friend.

"It is always good to see you here, Mr. Rollison. You are
well?" They exchanged pleasantries. Then : "Colonel White
is already here, he has a private room."

Private "rooms"—in fact, alcoves each with a heavy
curtain easy to draw—were usually reserved for those in
love; for couples who could not bear the contamination of
the gaze of ordinary, practical mortals. Or, as Rollison knew
well, for confidential discussions, often concerning large
sums of money, frequently in the shape and colour of dollar
bills.

The Colonel did not wish to be overheard.

The short man led Rollison up stairs which were narrow
and creaky, along a passage, into a room which was over the
shop next door and which had four curtained doorways. At
two curtains were drawn; one was empty; in the fourth,
sitting with a glass in front of him and a cigarette in a long
holder, was a man whom Rollison sensed he could like.

This man was massive, broad, not fat but fleshy. He had
a big, round face and round brown eyes. He looked the
kindly giant. Something in his manner, even while sitting,
said the same thing as his voice had said over the telephone;
he had an abounding vitality.

He sprang up.

"Rollison! Wonderful!" He came forward and pumped
hands. He had a powerful grip and approximated perpetual
motion. He drew Rollison into the little alcove and pushed
back his chair, offered cigarettes, lit one for Rollison. "Extremely good of you to come. Can't say how grateful we—I

am. Now, what will you drink? To start with, I mean—
we'll have one before eating. Gin? Whisky? Anything.
Name it."

"A dry Martini," said Rollison. "Thanks."

Service was beyond all words; perfect.

The drinks were mixed as by a genius.

The Colonel was something of a gourmet, and knew the
Gondoliers well; choosing their courses matched the per-
formance of ancient ceremonial rites. It was all very satis-
fying. It was also meant to induce in Rollison a proper and
receptive mood. One did not treat a stranger with such
selective generosity unless one had a substantial motive. Rollison was sadly sure that the Colonel was not behaving like
this simply out of the goodness of his heart.

"The soufflé," Wickford White said, "will be perfect."
Boyishly, he held up two fingers, close together, and clicked
his tongue. "Superb! After that . . ."

Over cigars and liqueurs he became a changed man.

"Rollison," he said when the curtain was drawn, "you
know our concern has a first-class reputation, don't you?
Value for money, everything of the best—don't feed our
guests quite like this, of course!"—he grinned expansively—
"but no one ever goes short of anything. When we say that
we give the best holiday value in the world, that's what we
mean. It wouldn't be your idea of a perfect holiday, but—
the thing is, we depend on a good reputation. We have to
maintain it. Can't let anything go amiss. Well, something *is*
going amiss at our Camp in North Wales. Huge place, we
can accommodate nearly six thousand people there. Vast.
And we're worried about it, very worried indeed."

His brown eyes were earnest.

His big hands were bunched on the table.

"We've told the police," he went on, "but they say there's
nothing much they can do about it. I suppose they're right,
but—well, let me make myself quite clear. A lot of people
wouldn't worry a tinker's cuss about this, but we're different.
Everything has to be just right. Our staff—Camp staff, I
mean—have to know everything that's going on. They pre-

tend not to notice a lot, but believe me there isn't much they miss. We take every precaution to make sure that things go smoothly. And without making a lot of fuss, too. One year we had trouble with some sneak-thieves, but settled it with our own Security people. We're on excellent terms with local people at all the Camps, and——"

He broke off.

Rollison did nothing to encourage him to continue the build-up. He had probably established what he wanted to establish—the importance of what he was about to say about Butlin's and was obviously giving Rollison time to digest all this.

Rollison drew at his cigar, sipped his liqueur, and hoped that he looked sufficiently wise.

His mind was empty of prejudice, but full of admiration for the Colonel's stage management.

"*Three* members of the staff at Pwllheli have disappeared," the Colonel announced, and paused again, to make sure that the statement sank in.

He succeeded in stirring the Toff to mild excitement, then leaned across the table and went on in a conspiratorial voice : "*Three*. They've vanished, without any reason at all. They were working happily, as far as we know, and then— well, poof, they disappeared ! No one saw them go, no one knew they were going. It was a vanishing trick which staggers us. By us," he added, as if there could be any doubt, "I mean Mr. Butlin and *all* the headquarters staff at Pwllheli."

"Male or female vanishers ?" asked Rollison.

"Male. All Redcoats, they——"

"Redcoats ?"

"Of course, you don't know. 'Redcoats' is the name we give a section of the staff at the Camps. You might say they're the members of the staff who keep the Campers happy. They wear red coats," added the Colonel, as if that explained everything clearly.

"I see."

"We've some all-the-year-round Redcoats, doing various

jobs in winter, but most work only for the season. Some come year after year. Some are university students, glad to earn a bit of ready in the long vac. They have to be able to get along with others, good at organizing games, running sports, keeping the party going. You'll see what I mean when you get there," the Colonel added, masterfully.

"When and where?" asked Rollison, who was in a remarkably subdued mood.

"I'm running ahead of myself, aren't I?" said the Colonel, and grinned. "Another liqueur? . . . Well, if you're sure, all right . . . Now what we want you to do is trace those three missing Redcoats. You'd have to come to the Pwllheli Camp for a week or two. Don't see how else you could do it," added the Colonel. "Do you?"

"Tell me more," invited Rollison.

"There isn't much more we can tell," said the Colonel. Suddenly, he looked worried. "The first chap disappeared early in April. At Easter. We were puzzled, but didn't do much about it. The Camp was pretty full, everyone was busy, one Redcoat more or less didn't make much difference, although Jim Campion was very popular. He's been with us all the winter, too—helping to get the Camps ready, arranging programmes—it's a huge undertaking, you know. Six Camps, half a million Campers a year. Think of the catering! Well, Campion just walked out, without saying a word to anyone."

The Colonel paused, to light his cigar. The flame flickered on his huge brown eyes.

"Then in the first week in June, the same thing happened with Tommy Tucker—real name Ernest, but everyone called him Tommy. That really started us thinking, because Tommy had been with us for seven seasons, on the regular staff, likely to go a long way in the organization. Exactly the same thing happened. We reported it to the local police. They made some inquiries, and referred to Scotland Yard. When he lived at the Camp, though, Tommy had no other address. There was nowhere he was likely to go. His relatives couldn't explain what had happened. His affairs were in order—no

money troubles or anything like that. Same thing applied to
Jim Campion."

"Wife?" asked Rollison.

"Oh, no, single. Most of the Redcoats are—but not all.
Then, only last week, Billy Peverill vanished." The Colonel
leaned back and threw his arms up and outwards in a gesture of astonishment and despair which would have gone
down well in any presentation of Gilbert and Sullivan.
"Billy Peverill was *the* star man at Pwllheli. Been there
donkey's years! He was the second-in-command, officially,
of all the Redcoats at the camp, popular with everyone—
especially the Campers. When he vanished, and the Camp
Controller told me about it, I knew we'd have to start some
new line of inquiry. *We're* convinced that there's something
mysterious, beyond our understanding, going on up there.
Of course, the police can't do much—people do disappear.
I know that Jim Campion, Tommy Tucker, and Billy
Peverill are listed as missing, that's all. None went home.
None had any known troubles. Vanished without trace.
Packed their bags and went. I don't mind telling you," the
Colonel went on earnestly, "that we're very badly worried.
Especially Mr. Butlin. *He* thought of calling you in. You
will come and help, won't you?"

Rollison said mildly : "What else do you know?"

"Absolutely nothing."

"No suspicions?"

"Nothing."

"Three vanished Redcoats——" began Rollison.

"Rollison, I want you to understand this," said Colonel
Wickford White, very solemnly, "we are concerned about
the men, as men; we want to know what's happened to
them. We do not believe that any one of them would have
gone away willingly, without telling us beforehand. So that's
one side of the problem. The other is—where have they gone
and why? What's happening at the Camp? It's a mystery
which we must solve. But we're not at all sure that it's a
matter the police can handle—three men have gone off,
that's all. No crime has been committed as far as we know.

The police will do what they can, but can hardly spare men to investigate. It's obviously a task for a private investigator, and we want the best. That's you. You can name your own fee—that may seem a reckless offer, but we trust you to be reasonable—we shall meet all expenses and give you all the assistance we can." The Colonel gave a magnificent gesture. "*Will* you come?"

"What about my Cover Girl?" asked Rollison, with praiseworthy gravity.

"She's at the Camp at the moment," said the Colonel, a grin breaking out on his face, which, until that moment, had been almost too solemn. "She won our Beauty Princess Competition three years ago, could have gone on the films, anywhere—but preferred a job with us. Nothing swollen-headed about our Liz! You'll like her."

"I rather think I will," agreed Rollison, straightfaced. "Yes, I'll come, but you must be told the risks. I shall need my man Jolly. You may think that a Camp wouldn't be exactly my cup of tea, but Jolly will probably ruin the holiday of everyone he meets. He regards Holiday Camps as the absolute zero among places of amusement. He'll hate you, and everything concerned with it, and——"

"A lot of people talk like that before they get there," said the Colonel breezily. "A kind of snobbery, you might say. Why, even I didn't like the idea of working for Butlin's, but now I'm absolutely sold on the whole business! We'll fix your man."

"Be it on your own head," said Rollison soberly. "He'll arrange terms, by the way, as my Business Manager. If he's too expensive, let me know, and I'll try to persuade him to come down a bit. When do you want me to start?"

"If I had my way, you'd start today," said the Colonel. "We'll brief you about the Camp, then I'll come up and introduce you to the Camp Controller and——"

"Easy," counselled Rollison. "Might be better if I start as an unknown quantity. A Camper—or why not a Redcoat?" He felt inspired. "And supposing I spent a couple of days at one of the other Camps, to get the hang of things.

Man Jolly could come too. Then I'd be sent to Pwllheli as a relief man, and could be revealed as a kind of Camp efficiency expert, if necessary. How does it sound for a start?"

"Wonderful," breathed the Colonel. But he looked not so much solemn as grave; troubled. Rollison could almost imagine that he was really touched by fear. "It's extremely important, old boy. Three missing Redcoats—sometimes I feel scared myself. What's happened to them? Are they"— he gulped—"alive or dead?"

"That's what we're going to find out," said Rollison firmly.

An hour later found him at New Scotland Yard, in the office of that tall, sallow, brown-eyed, and patient man— Superintendent Grice. Grice had learned to be long-suffering, even with the Toff.

He listened.

"I've heard a little about this," he admitted. "There's nothing yet to suggest there's any crime involved—which doesn't mean that I can be sure there isn't. They were all single chaps, with few belongings, no obligations except to Butlin's." He paused. "Are you going?"

"I think so."

"I must warn the Pwllheli police," Grice said dryly. "They'll need a couple of extra men to keep an eye on you."

The Toff beamed . . .

When he left, he was reasonably sure that the police did not take the disappearances seriously. Certainly they did not share Colonel Wickford White's fear that the missing men might be dead.

CHAPTER III

THE CAMP

ROLLISON drove an old Austin Sixteen, bought for the occasion and with a surprising turn of speed, along the winding Welsh road. Criccieth was behind him, before long he would be at the Pwllheli Camp. Behind him was everything he had learned during three days at the Camp at Filey, in Yorkshire; about the way Camps were run, and what was likely to happen. It had been a period of intensive training, and he regarded himself as now fully qualified as a Redcoat—save for one thing.

Experience.

Jolly had been with him, and had gone ahead to the Pwllheli Camp.

Nothing in this world would have made Jolly enthuse over the prospect of working at Butlin's; but the large fee had made him willing.

Rollison watched the green hedges, thick with summer's leaf; the bright green of the fields, the grey stone walls which divided fields from fields. Here and there was a stone cottage, with a tiny garden. He could see the sea between gaps in the hedges; it was warm and beautiful, and the countryside was at its best.

He felt relaxed.

The Camp Controller and one or two other senior members of the staff knew why Rollison was going to the Camp, and knew his real name.

He would be known as Richard Ryall.

As soon as he reached the Camp, he would report to the Entertainment Manager, in charge of Redcoats, and be given his duties. He had no idea how long he would need to remain anonymous.

Rollison passed beneath a bridge, made an S turn because the road became even more twisting just past the bridge, then came upon the Camp.

Rollison could see it for some distance. A row of flags, fluttering in the breeze, stood high above the road bordering the Camp itself. Beyond the road was a shrubbery; beyond that two swimming-pools, each with a diving-platform; beyond those, several buildings, brightly painted. These buildings, the dining-halls, shops, theatre, and ballrooms hid the rows of chalets where the Campers slept.

Rollison grinned to himself.

He wondered what Jolly had thought when he had arrived here; for at the Yorkshire Camp Jolly had become more and more dejected.

A mass of people were in or round the sides of the swimming-pools. The water seethed. At one end children, from toddlers upwards, ran, jumped, splashed, and shouted. Fond parents watched. Divers dived from high boards and low, and from the sides. The deep laughter of merriment floated across the warm July air.

Rollison found himself smiling.

He drove to the gates, and was stopped by two uniformed gate-keepers, given directions, and drove on.

The large buildings on this road, which ran parallel with the swimming-baths and the lawns and shrubberies at either end, were all clearly named. There were KENT HOUSE, PRINCES, EMPRESS, GLOUCESTER, the MIRROR BAR; and farther along, RECEPTION and OFFICES. Each building had a mass of windows. Roads led off the one along which Rollison drove and led to the chalets, which he could now see behind thick shubberies. His impression was of bright colours; both paint and Nature's. There were flowers everywhere; and chairs, tables, shops—everything—seemed to be red, blue, green, and yellow.

The sun burned down out of a clear sky.

Rollison pulled up outside OFFICES, and parked the car. The shrieking delight of the children sounded in a new crescendo when the car engine fell silent. He watched a girl standing on the high platform, nearly opposite, against a background of mountains.

She did a double somersault, and cleft the water smoothly.

"Nice-work," murmured Rollison. "Nice figure!"

As he reached one of the doors leading into the offices, Rollison heard a loud-speaker; and paused. The voice came from above him, and the girl spoke clearly.

"Hallo, Campers, this is Radio Butlin's calling." She paused. *"It is half-past four, and we want to remind you of the evening's programme. But before that, we can tell you that visibility is perfect—and conditions for flying couldn't be better! So why not see this wonderful camp from the air —as well as lovely Cardigan Bay, the Welsh coast, and all the beauty of the countryside?*

"Free transport will take you straight to the airfield at four-forty-five and again at seven-thirty, after dinner. If you haven't yet had this wonderful flight, now is the time.

"Dinner, of course, is at six-thirty. Then for tonight . . ."

Rollison moved towards the door, and three girls came out. At first sight, they looked almost identical. They had bright yellow hair, bright, sun-bronzed faces, yellow T-shirts moulded to quite outstanding figures, and short white pants which showed equally remarkable legs. They all had blue eyes. They all looked at him as if at some fabulous film star.

He may not have known what was passing through their minds, although in all likelihood he did.

He was dressed in a blue blazer, a loosely tied silk muffler, white flannels with a razor-edge crease, and a white shirt. He might in fact have been a film star on holiday.

As he passed them, he winked.

He heard one go: *"Oooooh!"*

He strolled into a big, square hall. On one side was a snack-bar; at the far end was a long counter; at the sides were counters marked KEYS and INQUIRIES. He marched straight to the long counter, past tables and chairs painted yellow, green, blue, and red. A big clock pointed to four-thirty-five.

Two girls were at the counter; they watched him, and smiled a welcome.

"I don't know if this is the right place," he said. "I have to see Mr. Middleton."

"Oh, a *Red*coat," said one of the girls, and looked delighted. "Yes, this is right, I'll show you his office." She pointed. "Go round that way, will you?"

Rollison did.

They met at the end of the counter, and the girl led him along passages between glass-walled offices. Dozens of people were busy in these, typewriters were clicking, comptometers working, people stood or sat at telephones.

He almost missed a step.

Jolly was sitting at a desk, with a nice-looking middle-aged women talking to him. Even that brief glimpse suggested that she had already acquired a possessive manner towards Jolly. They sat before a huge ledger; she appeared to be lecturing. Jolly looked forlorn.

"Here we are," said the girl, and tapped on a door which was already open. "Dick, here's someone to see you."

"Dick" Middleton was sitting at a desk at the far end of a small office. He was a dark-haired, fresh-faced man with plump cheeks and blue eyes; they were rather lack-lustre. He wore a red coat, with braid at the sleeves, a row of Camp badges on his coat lapel, and a thoughtful look.

"Who?" he asked.

"My name is Ryall," Rollison lied amiably. "Richard Ryall. I'm told——"

"Oh, the new chum," said Middleton, who was in charge of Redcoats. He didn't get up; he didn't look particularly enthusiastic or, for that matter, hostile. "Come to show us what we're doing wrong?"

"Don't let me fool you," Rollison said. "I just needed a job, and persuaded the Colonel that I was that good."

Middleton laughed, a little reluctantly.

"You have to be good, to get past him. Okay, May, thanks. Better come and sit down, Ryall. I'm busy for a minute, won't be long."

There were a dozen chairs round the walls. Rollison sat

down. Two men Redcoats came in within two minutes, nodded, put something on the desk, and went out. A girl wearing a red coat appeared, dropped a sheaf of papers on Middleton's desk, and went off, casting a glance at Rollison.

Middleton finished what he was writing.

"Sorry," he said, casually. "Well, now you're here, you'd better start learning the ropes. You've been to Filey, I'm told."

"For a little while."

"We aren't the same as Filey," said Middleton. "Not in our internal organization, anyway. For the first day or two, you'd better take it easy. Let me give you a tip—don't start throwing your weight about."

Rollison was beginning to doubt whether he would ever like Mr. Middleton very much.

"For some crazy reason, you're to team up with Liz Cherrell," Middleton went on. "She'll be in soon, and will show you round. I——"

He broke off.

A little man, wearing one of the red coats which were now becoming familiar, came breezing into the office. He wasn't much taller than Rollison's shoulder. He had a long, curved chin and a long, curved nose; he was a caricature of a caricature of Mr. Punch, and his cheeks were red as if they had been rouged. He had a slightly humped back, too—it might have been kinder to say that he had very round shoulders. His long dark hair was brushed straight back from his forehead, and his eyes were very large and brown; rather like the Colonel's.

He had a small, well-shaped mouth.

Two small boys, of perhaps six or seven, and a small girl with pig-tails, came after him.

"Damn it, Pi, can't you keep the kids out of the office?" complained Middleton.

"Won't be a jiffy," said the Punch of a man. His shrewd eyes turned towards Rollison; he smiled. "My fans follow me everywhere! Dick, I've got a hundred and seventy-one under-fives this week, and I'll have to have some more help in the afternoons. Just have to, or I can't manage 'em. Sorry."

Middleton's gaze immediately flashed to Rollison.

"That would give you an insight into the Camp," he said dryly. "Ryall, this is Peter Wray, called the Pied Piper here, or Uncle Pi. He's the Uncle to all the kids, and we're swamped with kids this week."

The Pied Piper grinned at Rollison.

"New Chum?"

"Yes."

"Must have upset our Dick," said the hunchback, "or he wouldn't have wished you on to me. Still, he's right—you don't know the camp until you've helped to entertain the under-fives! Okay, see you later. I've got to go and get rid of the mob outside," he added, and hurried out, calling over his shoulder : "Thanks, Dick."

The two boys and the small girl followed him gravely.

Rollison looked out of the window, and saw a group of thirty or forty young children. 'Uncle Pi' Wray walked along the road leading towards a bridge which Rollison could see in the distance. The children followed him—all shapes and sizes, tinies and early teen-agers.

"Amazing what he can do with kids," said Middleton. His admiration sounded reluctant. "I'll bet you won't be able to compete with him! Kids drive me crazy. Last man who helped Uncle Pi was Peverill, and the kids drove him out of the Camp!"

He gave a twisted kind of grin.

Then a girl wearing a red coat came in.

"Hallo, Liz," he said, "you're late." He seemed to be complaining, but now spoke with obvious restraint, as if he could not be natural with the girl. "Here's the new man we've had foisted on us, you're to hold his hand—but not too tightly, or there'll be some riots !"

The girl smiled.

She looked as if she had walked off the cover of the pamphlet; she was the Cover Girl come to life.

CHAPTER IV

LIZ

"Don't be too hard on Dick Middleton," said Elizabeth Cherrell.

She was walking with Rollison away from his car and towards the chalets. There were rows and rows of these, with green lawns between each row, flowers and bushes everywhere, huge hydrangeas outside most of them. The chalets were painted different colours; the roofs were multi-coloured, too.

Elizabeth Cherrell wore a pleated white skirt of knee length; no stockings on nice legs, white tennis shoes, a white shirt, and the red coat, and she walked with easy grace.

She looked earnestly at Rollison, who did not object.

"Why not?" he asked, shifting a suit-case from one hand to the other.

"He's had a lot of trouble lately. His wife ran away from him during the winter, and——" Elizabeth broke off. "It's soured him."

"Could being soured have driven her away?"

"No, he's a different man this year," said Elizabeth. "He was all right last year—otherwise the men would tear a few strips off him!" She smiled, but wasn't too happy about Middleton—she talked too much about him, suggesting personal interest. "He doesn't know who you are, of course."

"I should hope not. Our secret, yours and mine, and a few of the V.I.P.s. May I call you Liz, too?"

"Everyone else does."

"Elizabeth," said Rollison promptly, "friend Middleton let an interesting cat out of the bag just now. The last man to vanish was Peverill—and he was also the last man to help Uncle Pi. Did you know him?"

She didn't answer.

"Know Uncle Pi?" asked Rollison.

"*Everyone* knows Pi," Elizabeth's eyes glowed, making Rollison reflect that they were quite the most beautiful eyes he had seen for at least a year.

She spoke nicely, too.

"There's an Uncle at each Camp, to organize things for the children," Elizabeth said, "and I've known a lot of them—there's *never* been one anything like Uncle Pi. The children will follow him everywhere. He can't escape from them, they always manage to dig him out."

They were walking along a chalet line. Two or three people watched them. A fair-haired man followed, at a distance. They passed doors marked *Lassies* and *Lads* and the open door of a furnace shed, where a man was stoking the fire to heat the water in this line of chalets. Here and there swim-suits or towels, oddments of clothing, hung on improvised washing-lines.

"Your chalet's in the next row—the end one," said Elizabeth. The sun turned her hair to gold. "Chalet twenty-one, Row J. And your assistant, Mr. Jolly, is Chalet twenty-one, Row K—that's backing on yours. There's a communicating door."

"Wonderful," said Rollison.

"Here's your key," Elizabeth said.

They reached Chalet 21. The door was locked. Rollison put his case down, took the key, and opened the door.

"I think the best thing is for you is to have a wash and then have dinner," Elizabeth went on. "I can introduce you to some of the other Redcoats afterwards, and we can go round to the rest tonight. It would be a good way to show you round the camp, too."

"Couldn't be better," agreed Rollison. "But Liz——"

She looked strangely subdued; almost grave.

"Yes?"

"You are going to help me, aren't you?"

"Of course. It's my job."

"Is that all? No pleasure in it?"

"I don't know," she said, very quietly. "I just don't know what to say. I don't think I'm going to enjoy snooping."

"But we aren't going to get far if you don't answer simple questions."

"Such as whether I knew Billy Peverill. Yes, I did."

"Why didn't you answer at first?"

She said: "Well, I couldn't make up my mind what to say. Of course, I know Billy—he was here all last year. Possibly the reason he left was because Dick Middleton needled him so much. Dick knew that Billy detested working with children, he was the last man on earth to be detailed to help Uncle Pi out. All the others——"

"The other Redcoats?"

"Yes. They think that Billy Peverill just got fed up, and walked out. He wouldn't want to tell anyone why he was going, he wasn't the type to complain about anyone. He'd think that the best thing to do was skip, and he skipped."

"What about Tommy Tucker?" asked Rollison.

"Well, Tommy was always a bit restive. It puzzled a lot of them, but that's all."

"Jim Campion?"

"Everyone was really surprised about Jim, but he was the first to go, and everyone was so busy rushing about that it's hard to think much about him. Jim was here once, and isn't now. That's all. With a fresh horde of Campers every week, and hardly a minute to call our own, we don't get a lot of time to brood," Elizabeth said. "Now I must go. I—*what* name are you using?"

"Ryall."

"No, the first name."

"Richard. It saved changing initials on clothes tabs and that kind of thing. Why?"

"There's no point in being called Dick," Elizabeth said, "it would only annoy Dick Middleton. Have you a second name?"

Rollison grinned.

"Let's make it Roland instead of Richard, and I'll be Rolly—with a short O."

Her eyes danced with his.

"That's just right, Rolly!" She moved away from the

door, but didn't go far. "Do you——" She hesitated, and he thought that she coloured, although the bright sky was behind her and it was dark in the chalet and upon her face. "Do you really think there's anything to worry about?"

"The Colonel does."

"I suppose that's answer enough," said Elizabeth. "What else do you want me to do?"

"Think over everything that Jim Campion, Tommy Tucker, and Billy Peverill had in common," Rollison said. "Such as a dislike of working with children, or dislike of Dick Middleton, or drinking at the same pub—and let me know any factor common to all three."

"All right," promised Elizabeth.

She smiled, and turned away.

Rollison went to the door and watched her. Whichever way one looked at Elizabeth Cherrell, she was beautiful.

He wondered why she didn't want to take her chances on the films. He wondered why she championed Dick Middleton. He wondered why she was worried and whether she had any reason for trying to make light of the disappearances.

She turned a corner.

Rollison went back into his chalet, and closed the door. Small red curtains were drawn at the two windows. He pulled one aside, and stood close to the wall, looking out. He was hardly the same man who had talked to the girl or winked at the trio; or smiled at Uncle Pi. The Colonel would not have recognized him.

Jolly would.

Jolly had seen that tension in him before; the tightening of his mouth, the brightening of his eyes.

He watched, as for prey.

A man walked past the chalets on the other side of a lawn which stretched between two rows. He walked slowly along the path which ran outside all the chalets. He glanced towards Rollison's chalet, and slowed down.

He had curly fair hair, brawny arms covered with a mat of the same kind of fair hair; brawny legs, with big calves.

He wore khaki shorts and a white T-shirt, and he smoked a pipe.

He disappeared.

Rollison opened the door and watched, without letting himself be seen, until the man was out of sight. Then he opened the door wider, and with daylight streaming in, began to unpack his case.

The chalet was roomy, clean, bright. There was a hand-basin, a hanging wardrobe, chest of drawers, a chair, and a small metal table.

He had plenty to think about.

Dick Middleton, who was so ill-tempered; Peverill, who had vanished after doing a "turn" with children; Elizabeth Cherrell; and last, but certainly not least, the curly-haired man. In fact, the curly-haired man was the most important.

He was an ex-convict, known to the police as well as to Rollison.

His name was Clark; Horace Clark. Or it had been.

.   .   .   .   .

The man known to the Toff as Horace Clark strolled past Rollison's chalet. He did not quicken his pace until he reached the end of the row. He turned, and then broke into a run.

He ran fast.

The chalet rows were divided by paths which led from east to west, cutting across the paths outside the chalets. After turning left three times, Clark was soon back near Rollison; keeping behind some flowering shrubs, he could see Rollison busy in the chalet.

He grinned to himself, as if satisfied that he had not been noticed.

He walked away, and made no attempt to hurry.

Ten minutes later he was in the Mirror Coffee Bar, near the swimming-pools. There, the crowds were as thick as ever, and the water splashed, the sun made it heavenly. Only a few people sat drinking tea or eating cakes or buns. Three girls in white smocks were behind the serve-yourself

B

counter; two others were collecting dirty cups and saucers from the tables, which were all gaily painted. The walls seemed to be made of mirrors. A girl sat at a piano, strumming away as if she had no audience; certainly she deserved none.

A man sat near the piano.

Clark joined him.

"Hallo, Cy."

"Doing all right, Horace?"

"Sure I'm all right," said Clark. He aped American phrases and even American accent; it was like nothing heard on the other side of the Atlantic Ocean, but it obviously gave him a lot of satisfaction. "It's the Rollison guy," he added, as he sat down.

"Sure?"

"Sure I'm sure. It's the ruddy Toff."

Cy did not respond. He was thin, and when sitting down looked as if he were unusually tall. His knees poked upwards, as if he had folded his legs. He wore grey flannels and a green shirt. His dark hair was very thick and wiry.

"He recognize you?" Cy asked, suddenly.

Clark shook his head. "Not on your life, Cy. He hasn't seen me for four years, wouldn't recognize me if we were face to face, you needn't worry." He began to fill his pipe. "What are you going to do?"

Cy did not answer at once.

Clark filled and then lit his pipe.

"Not a thing," Cy said. "Not yet. We've got more work to do. We can't get out until we've finished. Even if we could, I wouldn't. But we only need a few days. We can fool him, we can fool anyone, for that time. We've *got* to fool him. We can watch, make sure he doesn't get to anyone."

"Listen, fella," Clark said, "he's *good*. I know we don't have to be scared, but we don't have to pretend he's a sucker."

"We'll watch him," Cy said. "Don't lose your nerve."

"My nerve's okay," Clark said. He drew at his pipe, as if

to prove it. He looked calm enough; in fact, he was a merry-looking man, in repose. "Cy," he went on, "about dem three Redcoats."

"What about them?"

"Where are dey?"

"I'll look after my end of the business, you look after yours." Cy had a nasty look in his eyes, which were rather small and very dark brown.

"Cy," said Clark, while the pianist kept striking the wrong notes and the two girls made cups and saucers and plates clatter, "I want to know. They're okay, aren't dey? You haven't bumped dem off."

Cy didn't answer.

Clark's hand moved, and clasped Cy's wrist. It was a strong, powerful hand. He gripped the bony wrist tightly.

"You heard me," he said.

"I haven't done anything to them," Cy said. "Not yet. Not until we've finished. When it's all over and we can get away, who cares what happens to them? They'll be the only people who could name us, wouldn't they? So who cares if they feed the fishes? They'd go down deep." He laughed.

The pianist was trying to play, "*I'm gonna wash that man right out of my hair.*"

"So long as they're alive and kicking now," Clark said. "I don't want to stand a murder rap."

"Didn't I tell you?" asked Cy, impatiently. He looked weak, against Clark, and his hand seemed white and frail, but he freed his wrist without any real effort. "Don't get funny, Horace," he said. "How about a shower before we eat?"

.   .   .   .   .

The two men had chalets near each other, in the same camp as the Toff. Clark left his, first, and the other joined him a few yards nearer the bath-houses. They disappeared. Rollison, watching from a corner and unseen by them, slipped across to the dark-haired man's chalet and looked through the window.

It was empty; but there were two beds, and a woman's dress hung over one.

The man would be away for ten or fifteen minutes at least, but the woman might be back at any moment.

Rollison took a pick-lock from his pocket; many cracksmen would have found the lock difficult to force, but he had it open in a trice. It was a trick of which the police disapproved. Someone came hurrying along the path, and Rollison stood with his face to the door, waiting; a youth passed.

Rollison went in quickly, closed the door, and went straight to the little chest of drawers. The oddments one might find in a married couple's room were here; clothing, toilet accessories, newspapers, magazines, make-up. None of these interested him. He glanced through the drawers, and found two letters addressed to :

Cy Beck Esq.,
c/o Butlin's, Pwllheli,
Wales.

Cy Beck . . .

The letters told Rollison nothing that he wanted to know. He put them back, then looked at the suit-cases, three of which were on top of a hanging wardrobe, two under one bed. Rollison dragged out one of these, and found it unlocked; so was the second; so were the three on the wardrobe. He found nothing else in which anything might be hidden, so he started to look in the suit-cases.

The third one he opened made him pause.

With a kind of sixth sense, he knew that he had found what he sought : a case which looked deep from the outside but was shallow inside; in short, one with a false bottom. He began to prod and probe the case, especially near the handle, until he found the spring control.

He was able to lift the lid of the false bottom.

He heard footsteps approaching, was ready to jump to his feet, but as he pulled at the lid, he felt a fierce sense of excitement.

The footsteps stopped.

Rollison let the lid fall, turned and faced the door, gritting his teeth. Then heard a key grate in the lock of the door of the next chalet. It slammed. He grinned, but felt himself sweating as he pulled the lid up, and looked down—at dollar bills.

There weren't really many; two small wads of fifty each; but each was for a hundred dollars, so this hoard was of five thousand dollars, not far short of two thousand pounds. The bills were all old and used; nothing suggested that they were counterfeit.

Rollison took one from each wad, slipped it into his pocket and closed the case. There was no need to relock it; the spring snapped into position. He straightened up.

He heard footsteps again.

He wanted to look for something else, to find out where Beck lived; anything; but this time the footsteps were a man's, and they stopped outside the door. Next moment, the key grated in the lock.

Rollison moved swiftly towards the door, getting behind it as it opened. He grabbed the bedspread off the bed. The door opened wide, and Cy Beck stepped in, obviously not giving a thought to the possibility that anyone was here. He didn't turn, just went forward, pushing the door behind him. Rollison flung the bedspread over his head and shoulders, then pinioned his arms in swift, planned movements.

He heard Beck gasp.

He felt the man's muscles tense, ready for an attempt to fight back. For a moment Beck tried to free himself with a desperate heave, but Rollison held him tightly and still more tightly, crushing him painfully.

Then he let him go.

People were passing to and fro outside; a woman was calling to a child.

"Be careful, Cy," Rollison said, clearly enough for the man to hear him. "You'll get yourself into trouble if you're not careful. And—you might get hurt."

He let Beck go, hooked the man's feet from under him,

broke his fall, then bundled him under the bed. Then he went to the door, opened it, and slipped outside.

No one saw him.

The woman was still calling to the child.

He hurried towards his own chalet, with the two $100.00 bills burning holes in his pockets.

CHAPTER V

SHADOWS . . .

ROLLISON heard footsteps outside the chalet, five minutes after he had returned, and started unpacking. He looked up; at Jolly.

He grinned a welcome.

"Hallo! Having a nice time?"

"I do wish you would leave the unpacking to me, sir," said Jolly, almost peevishly.

"Gladly. What do you know?"

"I can tell you to within a penny how much it costs to provide eighteen thousand meals for campers and six thousand for the staff each day," said Jolly, and shuddered. "And how long it takes to eat them, sir."

"Anything *important*?" asked Rollison, and there was a wicked gleam in his eyes.

"I am receiving a great deal of help, but I don't think that I have discovered anything which will assist us with the investigation," Jolly said, starting to pack shirts into a drawer. He had closed the door so that they could not be seen from outside. "One or two fancies have passed through my mind."

"There are a lot about," said Rollison, straightfaced. "Wearing nicely-filled T-shirts or swim-suits."

"I have been trying to satisfy myself as to the reason for the organization's eagerness to find the three missing men," Jolly went on, ignoring this flippancy. "If we allow that there is some anxiety about them as individuals, I think we should also allow that there may be some stronger motive."

"Such as?"

"Is the organization afraid that it is being swindled, sir?" asked Jolly tentatively.

"They'd use accountants to find that out."

"I think we shall find that they are particularly anxious

to make sure that the disappearances have nothing to do with the accounts and supplies," Jolly said, as he finished the unpacking. "Is there anything more you require before dinner, sir?"

"Yes."

"May I ask what it is, sir?" Jolly's startled tone showed that his question had been purely rhetorical.

"I want to know what Curly Clark is doing here," said Rollison. "Remember Curly? He served three years for a cat burglary—the few thousand pounds' worth of jewels he pinched were never recovered. He's been out for a year or so —and he's here, a bosom friend of a man who could be an Old Testament prophet beloved by Lucifer. We'd better find out who they meet, what they're doing, how long Clark's been here. We'll soon have to decide whether to use the Camp Security men or manage on our own, too. I'll have a word with the Camp Controller."

"Among six thousand people, you are bound to have one or two old lags, sir," Jolly reasoned.

"That's reasonable. But this one followed me first. Then he met a man named Cy Beck, who had two thousand dollars in the false bottom of his suit-case in Chalet K34," went on Rollison brightly. "Now shout currency racket at me."

"I *see*," said Jolly, in a very respectful tone.

"Remember Clark?" asked Rollison.

"*Very* well, sir."

"I shouldn't think he saw much of you. We'll let them sweat for a bit, but haunt Clark's chalet, and find out what you can about his boy friends—including Cy Beck."

"I most certainly will," promised Jolly.

He went through the communicating door to his own room. He seemed dazed, although in fact nothing the Toff did would ever really surprise him.

Rollison, still content, washed, and looked at his watch; it was a quarter to six. He turned towards the door, and someone tapped; it was a small youth, carrying a bright-red coat on a hanger.

"Mr. Ryall?"

"That's right."

"Yer coat," said the youth. "Mr. Middleton says he forgot to tell you about it."

"Oh yes," said Rollison. "Thanks."

He put it on. He had known poorer fits. He went out, feeling unexpectedly self-conscious. He grinned to himself, to the obvious delight of several girls. Two stood in their doorways, watching him. But no men followed him—yet.

He expected reprisals soon.

At the road at the top of the chalet lines, he turned right, towards a water-tower with huge toy soldiers at each corner—giants who gazed benevolently down on a children's playground. There, swings, roundabouts, see-saws, and contraptions of all kinds were being used with a kind of concentrated enjoyment by children from five up to fifteen. Wray, or the Pied Piper passed, with a crocodile of infants in his wake. He looked at the Toff. "No extra charge, but they still follow me. See you later." He hurried on.

Rollison entered the offices and found his way among glass-walled passages and nearly empty offices to a door marked : "Controller".

Two men were inside.

He tapped; they looked up, and one beckoned.

Rollison went in.

"Hallo, Mr. Rollison," said one of the men, rising from a large desk. He was short, spruce, and in some odd way, retiring. "I'm Captain Aird—I've been expecting you. This is Mr. Llewellyn, my assistant."

Llewellyn was a smaller, milder Colonel Wickford White, wearing a black-and-white check jacket.

"Hallo," said Rollison brightly. "My name's Ryall." He grinned as Aird waved him to a chair.

"How are you finding it?" Aird was dressed in brown, and had a quiet-speaking voice; he might be a brilliant administrator, but looked the last man in the world to be in command of a Camp. "Any villains in mind?"

"Four," said Rollison, carefully.

Aird was startled. "Seriously?"

"Half-seriously. There's a jewel-thief named Clark whom I'd like to know more about, and a friend of his. My man's after them, but I don't think he'll be able to manage for long on his own." Rollison accepted a cigarette, was very bland, gave no hint that he had a dollar problem and reason to suspect a motive. "Thanks very much." He lit it. "I think your Security fellows ought to come in, without being told what's on. We could be after a thief or a suspect."

"Of course," said Aird. "What's this Clark like?"

Rollison told him.

"Hardly likely that a jewel-thief would expect a picking here," said Llewellyn, sceptically. "Shall I tell the Security Officer about it, or would you like to work with him yourself?"

Aird made no comment.

"Oh, you for the time being," said Rollison. "I'll remain a Redcoat. Had any trouble with Middleton?" he asked casually.

Aird said slowly: "Yes and no. I'm told he's had a rough time domestically, and certainly he's a bit sour. We want to try to help him, so are letting things ride for a bit. If you mean do we think that Middleton knows anything about this—no, he's the last man I'd suspect."

"Why?"

Aird shrugged.

"The thing is," Rollison pointed out, "that Redcoats have to do what Middleton tells them, more or less. He could say: 'Meet me at the boating lake' or 'by the rock gardens', and the Redcoat would almost certainly be there, wouldn't he?"

"That's right," said Llewellyn, making a more hopeful contribution. "Hadn't thought of that."

"So one of the things we want to find out is whether Middleton saw each or any of the three who've disappeared, about the time they were last seen—and whether he gave them any special orders," Rollison said. "Also whether my villain Clark or anyone he knows at the Camp is acquainted with Middleton. There are two ways to handle this—Jolly and I alone, which would take a lot of time, or with help from you people. I rather lean towards help."

"I think you're right," agreed Aird. "I'll get moving."

"Another thing," Rollison murmured. "If all three Red-coats disappeared for the same reason—and under compulsion—the same individuals might have compelled them. That means any member of the camp staff who's been here since Easter—and also any Campers."

"Don't get many Campers coming more than twice a season, not many come twice," said Aird. "They have their week or fortnight's holiday, and that's that. Of course, we have daily visitors. We'll check."

"Thanks," Rollison beamed.

He went out, still resplendent in his red coat. There were crowds by the swimming-pool, but practically no children; it was getting near dinner-time. Gaily painted bicycles and tricycles were speeding about everywhere.

Clark was studying books in a shop window, but did not follow as Rollison walked slowly along this road, towards the entrance gates. He had to pass a huge dining-hall, GLOUCESTER—where he would eat. Waitresses were bustling about inside; the place looked colossal. He strolled past the Viennese Bar, which was open and busy, and was soon within sight of the gate-house.

Now he was being followed.

At first, he had only sensed it; now he was sure.

But it was by a girl, not a man.

She was probably in the early twenties; easy on the eye, and with quite a figure. She wore a cotton frock and a wide-brimmed straw hat, and white shoes. She walked well. Now and again, when Rollison paused at a shop window, she paused, too; but undoubtedly she was following him.

Rollison turned a corner opposite a building with display windows of photographs outside and the words PRINCES THEATRE blazoned over the front door. He stepped into the doorway of a sweet-shop, opposite, and the girl came round the corner. She had red hair, and he hadn't noticed that before; it wasn't very red, but deeper than gold.

She saw him, and missed a step.

"Hallo," he said, and beamed. "Lovely evening, isn't it?" She stopped.

"You—you *are* Mr. Rollison, aren't you? The Toff." The words came out with great difficulty; fearfully. "Aren't you?"

"Listen," Rollison said, "you can think what you like, but my name is Ryall. I'm a Redcoat here." He beamed at her again.

"You're—Rollison. I want——" She gulped. "I want to talk to you. I—must."

"What about?"

"I can't talk here." She looked over her shoulder. Several people were in sight, none seemed to take any particular interest in her—but Clark was at a far corner. That was more as Rollison expected—but had Clark seen the girl? "Can I—come to your chalet?" she asked.

"No." If this were genuine she might be followed to his chalet, and she wouldn't want that. If she were fooling him, she wouldn't care where they met. "Let's dance tonight, and you can tell me——"

"I *must* see you alone." Her eyes had green flecks in the gold. Did they tell of some inward terror? She wasn't beautiful in the sense that Elizabeth Cherrell was, but she had looks and everything. "I——"

The radio crackled, and a girl gave announcements clearly. This girl started violently, a fair indication of the state of her nerves. She looked nervously over her shoulder.

Clark had gone into a doorway.

"I mustn't stay here," she said urgently. "What's your chalet number—*please*?"

Clark came out of his doorway and walked off.

Rollison took a chance.

"J21," he said.

"Oh, thank you!" The girl hurried past, adding urgently: "I'm Susan Dell. I'll come when I can."

Had she really been scared, or had she been fooling him? Clark may have been watching to make sure she did her job. Rollison left the shop doorway and strolled towards the chalet lines. The radio girl spoke to the unseen multitudes.

"Just to remind you, Campers, that dinner will be ready in fifteen minutes—it's now six-fifteen. And for those of you who haven't yet seen the Camp from the air, or seen the beautiful Welsh coast, why not take a pleasure flight this evening? Visibility is perfect, you'll never have a better opportunity. Free transport will be provided . . ."

There were several other announcements; Rollison hardly noticed them. He kept thinking about the girl. He wished he knew whether, and if so why, she had been so frightened of being seen with him.

No one else had followed him, and he had seen no one follow her.

What use could she make of knowing his chalet number? Clark and his friends already knew it.

He went back to the chalet, told Jolly about the girl, and sent him off to his meal, promptly. He himself waited until a quarter to seven; no one turned up. He walked towards the dining-hall. A few other late Campers were hurrying near the huge room.

He went in.

A vast mass of people sat at the yellow, red, and blue tables; a thousand or more, with waitresses rushing from the big serving cupboards in the middle of the hall. At first it was overpowering; and hot beyond words. He heard people laughing; there was a background of talk; a satisfied kind of babble.

He tried to imagine Jolly in this.

Several other Redcoats were near the door, Uncle Pi was among them.

"Hallo." Uncle Pi's brown eyes were smiling and friendly. "Late tonight? Do you know where you're to sit?"

"Row A, I think, somewhere near the door."

"Oh, yes, Peverill's place." Uncle Pi pointed.

"Thanks," said Rollison.

He sat down in the place of a missing man. The place was at a table for four—with another table for four close to it.

Seven Campers, three girls, three young fellows, and a man with a grey beard and a silly smile, all grunted or smiled; and the girls glanced sideways at him. A waitress came rushing up.

"Hallo, dear, you're late," she said to Rollison. "Soup?"

"I'll miss it."

"Ta, ducky." She hurried off, to return with a plate of fish and chips; he expected to find it cold and unpalatable, but found himself enjoying it. A youth asked him if he knew what the Square Dancing would be like that evening.

"Championship stuff," Rollison said absently. He was looking about him, and caught sight of a head of fair, curly hair on a man sitting with his back to him; it might be Clark.

The girl by the man's side had hair that was red tinged.

He watched; he was worried about that girl.

The waitress gave him stewed fruit and custard. He was half-way through it when he saw the curly-haired man get up.

It was Clark.

He stood in the aisle by the side of his table and waited for the girl to get up, too.

A youth said something to Rollison again.

"Oh, yes," Rollison said. He glanced at the youth, then back at Clark and the girl. She was walking with Clark towards the door, and she was Susan Dell, who had followed him—and who had seemed so frightened.

She was frightened now. Her fear showed unmistakably when she looked at Rollison.

Clark glanced at her, and his hand closed over hers. There was something threatening in the movement. Rollison didn't like it at all.

He got up.

He reached the door as Clark and the girl reached the corner. He turned after them, and a man, coming from the other direction, banged into him. It might have been an accident, but it sent him reeling against the window.

Clark and the girl disappeared.

CHAPTER VI

MISSING GIRL

"Sorry, chum," said the big man who had cannoned into Rollison. "You okay?" He moved forward, full of solicitude, and gripped Rollison's arm. He was big, and brutish, bulky rather than fat, with a long nose which was pushed a little to one side, and big, rather prominent teeth. His grip was remarkably powerful. "Never saw you coming," he went on, and again hampered Rollison, who wanted to get to the corner. "Lemme brush you down, and——"

"I'm all right, thanks."

"No offence *meant*," said the bulky man with the big teeth. "'Aven't we met before?" His hand was enormous; fingers spanned Rollison's forearm.

He hurt.

This was the reprisal; or a form of one—Rollison was quite sure. Cy Beck didn't know, but he would guess who had been in his chalet, and was probably desperate to know if Rollison had seen the dollars.

This man was a powerful brute.

Rollison flexed his arm and twisted his wrist—and caught hold of the other man's. He twisted again. He saw the look of surprise and pain on the big face. He beamed.

"None taken," he said, and hurried to the corner. The big man was behind him, gaping. Two or three others watched.

Clark and the girl had vanished.

She had wanted to see him; she had come to him for help; and now he felt sure that she was frightened. It might have nothing to do with the missing men; it might have a great deal. There was more; the bulky man had been there to impede him, deliberately; Clark certainly wasn't by himself in this.

Clark had seen and recognized him—and was worried about him.

"Rolly," a girl called.

Only Elizabeth Cherrell would call him Rolly here; only Elizabeth had a voice like that. He turned. Seeing his expression, her smile faded.

It wasn't surprising. Clark had seen the girl talking to him, Clark was a villainous type. Beck *looked* murderous. It was vital to find Susan—because he had left her to her own devices.

But he fought back his fears.

"Hallo," he said to Elizabeth. "Gainsborough would have doted on you."

"What's the matter?"

"I was looking for a girl who's disappeared. Where do people go at this hour of the evening?"

"Almost—anywhere," she said. "One of the theatres, the games room, the quiet lounges, the coffee bars or the other bars. *Anywhere.*"

"Where will I find Llewellyn or Aird?"

"They're in their living-quarters, I expect—I'll take you there."

"Let's hurry," said Rollison. He took her arm; life had its compensations. "Can we go by car?"

"Part of the way."

He hustled her towards his car. People were thronging out of the dining-hall and towards the Princes Theatre and the licensed bars. He had never seen so many people about at the same time. Some were diving and swimming again.

He got into the old Austin, Elizabeth beside him.

As he drove off, Middleton appeared from a chalet. He stood staring.

"Redcoats aren't supposed to drive," Elizabeth said.

"Forget it," said Rollison. "Just direct me, will you?"

She told him where to stop—at the end of a road which had led past more big buildings and more chalet lines. Then they walked, Rollison outpacing the girl; she had to trot. At last they reached the living-quarters of Aird and the senior officers at the camp.

Aird was in his room.

"Hallo," he said, "I'm glad you've come. I—what's the trouble?"

"I'm just jittery. Any news of Clark?"

"You certainly got a move on," Aird said. "He's stayed at the Camp three times, twice for long week-ends, this time for two weeks. Each time, it's coincided with the disappearance of a Redcoat. He's come with a girl now, a red-head named Susan Dell. They've single chalets, not far from you."

"I'm worried about Susan Dell," Rollison said. "Will you tell the Security people to pick her up."

"Can we give any reason for——"

"We'll find a reason if we get her," Rollison said briskly. "She asked me for help, and I wasn't any." Eyes with green flecks drove him by a fear which infected the others. "Liz and I are also going to look."

"All right." Aird reached for a telephone.

"Rolly," Liz said, as they reached the car. "What *is* worrying you?"

"A pair of golden eyes with green in them," said Rollison. "Nearly as beautiful as yours. We'll have a drive round, and keep our eyes open for the pair. Can you drive?"

"Yes."

"Will you?"

"Yes." She took the wheel. She had nice hands, pink nail varnish, and was a natural driver.

He had studied the plan of the Camp, but it hadn't given him any real idea of the size. They seemed to drive for miles along well-made roads, now past chalets, tennis courts, playing-fields, over a railway bridge, past a boating-pool, within sight of the roller-skating rink; playgrounds; gardens. There were three chalet camps, each with its own roads, its own main buildings.

They covered every road.

Now and again Rollison saw a girl with red hair; once, a man who might have been Clark; it wasn't.

"Let's try the rock garden," Rollison said. "It's a place for canoodling and keeping out of sight. Then——" He broke off.

"There's the beach," Elizabeth said.

"Yes. Afterwards."

They pulled up by the entrance to the big rock garden which ran alongside the railway and the Camp station. Dozens of couples were sitting remote or indifferent on the benches or in alcoves; but not Susan Dell or Clark.

"How near the beach can we take the car?" The driving urge still forced Rollison.

"Not very near."

"How far is it to walk?"

"Ten minutes."

"Come on," he said.

When they got out of the car, the loud-speaker was on, and a girl's voice was coming towards them, but Rollison couldn't catch the words. They walked over uneven grass-land towards the sea. An aeroplane droned overhead. Soon, they were climbing over a rocky headland. From the top they could see the small beach, the boats drawn up, a few people bathing, dozens of couples sitting against the rocks.

Clark and Susan Dell weren't there, either.

"You're scaring me," Elizabeth said.

"I'm scaring myself." Rollison squeezed her arm. "Sorry. Let's go back."

They were near the Montgomery Theatre, in the South Camp, when Llewellyn pulled up just in front of them in his car, forcing them to stop. He got out. They met, between the two cars.

"Neither Clark nor the girl has been seen anywhere," Llewellyn said. "They haven't been seen to leave the Camp, but——"

"Easy enough to slip out if they want to, isn't it?"

"Oh, of course—but they weren't noticed."

"We'll keep looking," Rollison said.

"All right."

"They might be in one of the theatres," Elizabeth suggested. "The ballrooms aren't very full yet."

The hurried across to the theatre and went in; the Red-coat in charge put on the lights between two stage turns.

Every chair was occupied, and hundreds of Campers stood against the walls. Rollison walked down one side and up the other; he would have picked out the couple, if they had been there.

Outside, Elizabeth said : "Shall we try the ballrooms?"

"Yes."

They tried the ballroom here, then the huge one, in the West Camp. They tried the Princes Theatre, all the bars, everywhere.

They didn't find the man or the girl.

. . . . . .

Rollison felt bad; very bad. He was with Aird, Llewellyn, Elizabeth, and Jolly, in Aird's office. It was nine o'clock. There was still no news.

"Of course someone is going to say that they might turn up," he growled, "but who really believes it?"

Aird said : "They've packed their cases and gone. It's just like the others—they've vanished into thin air." He pulled at a pipe. "What are you going to do?"

"First, drop all pretence within the camp staff, I think. Let the Redcoats, Security chaps, and anyone else who can help know who I am and what I'm doing—ask Middleton to co-operate, too." His voice was cold, he looked bleak. "Please yourself whether you tell the Campers."

"We won't yet." Aird didn't like this.

"What is there to tell them?" Llewellyn demanded. "Two Campers have packed up and gone off. It's happened before." He didn't put his thought into words, but obviously doubted whether Rollison was justified in making a fuss.

"We've got to find Clark and that girl," Rollison said. "We've got to find all Clark's friends at the Camp, too." He wanted to deal with Cy Beck himself, for the time being; for more reasons than one. "Hell of a job, but—check at the snack-bars, other bars, dining-rooms, his chalet—find out if he or Susan Dell made any particular friends, and then run a ruler over them." He lit a cigarette. "Please."

"Look here——" Llewellyn began.

"They will pay me a fat fee," Rollison observed. "Let me earn it." He smiled, bleakly. "Come on, Liz." He took Elizabeth's arm and hurried out of the room, went back to the car, but didn't drive off at once, just sat smoking beneath a star-filled sky and within the sound of dance music.

"Where are we going?" Elizabeth asked.

"Clark's chalet," Rollison said. "We can get the key from Reception, can't we?"

"Oh, yes."

Clark's was a small, single chalet. It hadn't been tidied up, and the bed hadn't been made. There were several empty cartons, a box of matches, silver paper from chocolates, and other oddments—including two hair-grips, obviously meant for red hair. There was a dusting of powder over the chest of drawers which also served as a dressing-table.

"Susan made up here, in a hurry," Rollison said. "Liz, they were ready to leave—or Clark was—before they came in to dinner. She must have left me, and then gone back to her chalet and packed. She was frightened out of her wits." He led the way out of the chalet; no one was about. "When in doubt, have a drink. Which is the nearest bar?"

"The Viennese."

"Come on, then."

He had a drink; he had another drink; then he had a drink. Elizabeth made one last for the duration. Now and again Rollison reminded himself that she was as beautiful as her picture, that she had a mind, that it would be easy to grow very fond of her. More often, he was thinking of Susan.

The bar got noisier, the smoke grew thicker, then crowds came out of a theatre.

"Let's get some air," Rollison said.

He led the way. A middle-aged woman, with greying hair and a glass of beer in her hand, stood up from a table as he passed her. He jogged her arm, slightly. The glass fell, beer splashed.

"Oi, you clumsy brute," she spat, and spun round on

him. She was flushed, she had a big, loose, wet mouth. "See what you did, knocked it aht of me 'and, you——"

"I know 'ow to deal wiv *that* kinda mugger," a man said.

His voice was familiar. He was big, with large and rather prominent teeth. He and Rollison had met outside the dining-hall. He swung his right, and if the punch had landed, it would have sent Rollison flying.

It missed.

Something in the man's manner told the truth; he was here to beat Rollison up; and he had a brute's strength.

"Rolly!" cried Elizabeth.

The woman with the loose mouth pushed her out of the way, as the bulky man smashed another blow at Rollison.

CHAPTER VII

DRUNK?

THE second blow missed.

Someone shouted: "Pack it up." He was wasting his breath. The bulky man pushed a table aside, so as to get at Rollison. His eyes were quite clear, he wasn't drunk, but he bellowed as if he were, and hiccoughed as he made a lunge at Rollison.

He was good, too.

He got through Rollison's guard with a heavy blow over the heart. He swung the next low. Then he brought his knee up, but Rollison dodged in time. Men were shouting, women screaming, Redcoats came rushing.

Rollison closed with the bulky man.

He thought he distinguished Elizabeth's voice: *"Be careful!"*

He had met giants like this before. He jolted the man with a right to the chin; they grappled; then he gripped the other man's right wrist. He hurt.

He seemed to make no great effort, but the man went flying, and fell against two Redcoats who were almost in the fray. It was quite a moment, undoubtedly a sight worth seeing. Three tables, nine glasses, and five ash-trays crashed, with Redcoats and the bulky man on top of them, and a dozen others rushing to get out of the way.

Rollison dusted his hands.

That made a youth laugh. Others laughed with him, glad of relief from tension. Rollison grinned about him. Men and women, scared the moment before, or at least anxious to avoid trouble, were chuckling. Only some bruised and damaged Redcoats, Elizabeth, the bulky man, and the loose-mouthed woman weren't smiling. The woman was glaring at Rollison in a way which could only be called unpleasant.

She went to her champion.

"Nice work, Ryall," said Uncle Pi. He came from one side. "I haven't seen——"

"Nice work be damned!" That was Middleton, from behind Rollison. He clutched Rollison's shoulder and spun him round. His face was livid, he looked as if he were glaring at a man he hated. "Take that coat off, Ryall," he growled. "You're suspended until this has been reported."

"Dick——" began Uncle Pi.

"You shut up!"

Rollison glanced round. There were a dozen Redcoats within sight, and more were coming in; they appeared with the remarkable instinct of London policemen at a street accident. Those who were nearer showed no liking for Middleton. Middleton himself looked as if he expected to be defied.

Rollison said : "All right, Middleton." He took his coat off, emptied the pockets, and turned away.

Two Redcoats were helping the bulky man to his feet. His lips were bleeding.

"You know, Dick, it wasn't the Redcoat's fault," said an elderly Camper, obviously anxious to pacify. "It was the other chap, he was drunk. I saw——"

"Any Redcoat ought to be able to keep clear of drunken brawls," Middleton said savagely. "The moment I looked at you, Ryall, I thought the kids were more your mark. Understand, you're suspended, until——"

"Dick——" began Elizabeth.

"Oh, you'll try to whitewash him," Middleton sneered. "He didn't take long to put you in his pocket."

Campers looked troubled. Elizabeth flushed, and turned away. Rollison didn't follow. Uncle Pi went up to Middleton, and whispered something which made him move towards the doors. Other Redcoats were tidying the place up, with help from waitresses and willing Campers. Someone at the far end of the bar began to sing.

Rollison went out.

He was hot; and the night air stung his forehead, face, and body. Some way off, Middleton and Uncle Pi were talking beneath a light, but Elizabeth wasn't in sight. Rollison walked briskly towards his own chalet line; he needed a coat.

Middleton had been theatrical in his rage, and true rage wasn't often theatrical.

Had the man been acting a part?

Did he hate?

If he already suspected what Rollison was doing, and if he were working with the men who had made three Redcoats disappear, hatred would be understandable. He was sour, bitter, difficult to get on with. The reason seemed good enough; but supposing he were under some other kind of pressure.

Rollison reached his chalet.

He opened the door, and Jolly called out from the chalet at the rear:

"Is that you, sir?"

"And in one piece," said Rollison. He put on the light, and studied his face in the mirror. There was a promising bruise on his right temple; that was all. He put on his coat, as Jolly appeared, having smoothed down his hair. He was in his blue-and-white spotted dressing-gown. "Fight," Rollison said, "with a man who seemed drunk. Or pretended to be drunk."

Jolly said: "Indeed, sir?"

"Big, bulky chap, who'd already stopped me from following Clark and the girl," Rollison said. "We don't like him, do we?"

Jolly didn't speak.

"We aren't exactly bosom friends with Middleton, either," Rollison added, "and now I suppose I'd better sit down and tell you what's been happening."

He talked, at some length. Much of what he said was highly speculative, some was even ornamental. But it cooled him down. Cool, he realized how furious he had been with the bulky man, because of fears for the missing Susan Dell.

"It would appear that the man who feigned drunkenness wanted to incapacitate you," Jolly said, as if all had been revealed to him.

"Or put it another way," Rollison said. "Beat me up and warn me off, and all lush apology in the morning for having been blind drunk. We'll search his chalet before long. We'll also have a look at Middleton's." A glow came to his eyes, a mellowness to his voice; he was no longer filled with rage. He actually smiled. "I think we can see a little daylight, Jolly. We have to be careful with the Bulky One, and not warn him off—he'll lead us where we want to go. I think. I——"

There were footsteps; light and quick, those of a woman. They stopped.

There was a tap at the door.

Jolly slipped into his chalet, and closed the door. Rollison glanced out of a window which was slightly open, and saw Elizabeth's fair hair. He opened the door. She was ready with words as soon as she saw him.

"Rolly, did he hurt you?"

"Think nothing of it," said Rollison, and stood aside. "One honourable scar and a clear conscience. How do I do as a knight errant? Come in."

She came in. She looked agitated.

"Rolly, Dick wants to apologize. Will you let him? Before he knows who you are, I mean. If he apologized afterwards it wouldn't really mean much, would it?"

Rollison said gently : "Elizabeth the Kind-Hearted. Don't fight too many battles for Dick Middleton, sweet Liz, or you'll be in trouble yourself. Of course I'll see him—but I shouldn't urge him to come, if I were you. He——"

"He's coming," Elizabeth said. "Uncle Pi and some of the others convinced him about what really happened."

"Good. Where's Uncle Pi?"

"With Dick."

"He has a way with young men as well as children," Rollison murmured. "I want to know all about the chap who was drunk, Liz, because I don't think he was half as drunk as he made out."

She looked at him, round-eyed. They were the loveliest eyes he had seen for at least eighteen months. They were set in the loveliest face. A shadow of doubt, much smaller than a man's hand, crossed his mind about her; not about her goodwill, but about her level of intelligence. Was she—could she be—just a little dumb?

"Oh, you see evil in everything!" she exclaimed.

She turned on her heel. He reached the door before her, and bowed slightly. Head high, she went out. He closed the door again and scratched his head. He went to the telephone, called Llewellyn, told him what had happened, and asked for information about the bulky man; especially his chalet number. Llewellyn had already heard of the fracas.

"Are you sure you're all right?"

"Positive," Rollison said. "And while you're finding out what you can about the chap, will you——?" he paused.

"Yes?"

"Forget it." Rollison changed him mind. "I don't want to give you a lot of work for nothing. Thanks."

He rang off, sat on the side of his bed and contemplated the wall opposite. It was apple green with one or two slightly darker patches. He lit a cigarette. He got up, opened the top drawer of the chest, and took out one of the pamphlets with Elizabeth Cherrell's photograph on it. He found two pins and pinned the photograph to the wall, then went back and stared at it. The wall, in fact the room, looked a brighter, lovelier place; a thing of beauty.

He winked at her.

There was a tap at the communicating door, and on his "come in" Jolly entered. Jolly wore a black-and-white check coat, flannels, and a white scarf. His cheeks were flushed, and his eyes were bright; he looked almost a happy man.

"My, my," breathed Rollison, "who is she?"

Jolly had a mind as quick as any rapier, and he had seen the picture on the wall. He did not smile, but said gravely: "Miss Cherrell, I believe, sir—Miss Elizabeth Cherrell. I have just been out for a walk before retiring. Cy Beck is married, has been here a week, and was here when Clark was in the Camp before, too. That's all I know yet, sir."

Rollison contemplated him in thoughtful silence; and gradually became sombre. For a few minutes, that driving fear for Susan Dell had left him; Elizabeth had driven it away. Now, it came back. It was not so urgent, because he knew there was nothing that he could do about it immediately; but it would be in his mind until he had found the girl with red hair and green flecks in her eyes.

"Progress of a kind," he said. "And we must check Middleton, and find out if any of the missing Redcoats knew Beck or Clark."

"Naturally, sir."

"And we must check Miss Cherrell."

"Of course," said Jolly.

"Why of course?"

"There is some measure of affection between Middleton and Miss Cherrell. I discovered from one of the ah—clerks —in the offices that last year they were very close friends then. *Very* close friends."

"Oh," said Rollison, and rubbed the tip of his nose with his forefinger. "Were they? And Miss Cherrell resented it because I've shown some doubts about Middleton. Do you think it could have been a mistake to have her as guide and counsellor?"

"It may have been, sir, but there was no way of anticipating it."

"Consolation. Jolly, did anyone tell you that three Redcoats have disappeared? That is to say, Camp officials. I mean," he went on, as if he were a child making a wild guess at some improbable question, "friends of people like Middleton, Uncle Pi, and Elizabeth Cherrell. We saw the obvious possibility that Middleton might be involved because he's in a position to give the other Redcoats orders, didn't we? Therefore, we can't trust Middleton. We can't trust any of the officials, either. Aird, I suppose, and Llewellyn—but no absolute certainty about any of them. If this thing is big enough to warrant Clark smuggling Susan Dell out of the Camp in a hurry, it might be very big. Dollars are involved. We could act too quickly—and we could tell the wrong people what we know, couldn't we? After all, this could involve those in high positions. Agree?"

Jolly was just himself : "I do indeed," he said.

"Or to make it simplicity itself, we can't afford to trust anyone."

Jolly didn't speak this time.

"Clark and Beck were here at the time of each disappearance. Think you can find out if anyone else was?"

"I'm quite sure I can," Jolly said, and there was positive eagerness in his eyes. "I find the staff most co-operative."

"Obviously. Your job," Rollison said dryly. "Tomorrow." He regarded his man coldly, and with some suspicions. He had never seen Jolly in quite such a mood. In spite of the situation, he recognized the kind of mood in which he might burst into a laugh, or wear a button-hole, or even blow a tin trumpet. Jolly's expression was almost smug. "Good night," Rollison said.

"Good night, sir," said Jolly. He smiled broadly. "I hope you sleep well."

He went out, bowing slightly before he closed the door. After a moment, there came a sound—an unusual sound, a lilting humming of a sound. Jolly, giving his rendering of *La Ronde*.

Jolly, *gay*—at this place !

It was so improbable here that it was hard to believe. To make it worse, it was a mood which Rollison could not capture. He lit another cigarette and stared at Elizabeth. Her beauty was sufficient to befuddle any man. He disliked his doubts about her; he also disliked the way she had flared up. He thought that if she loved a man, she would do anything to help him.

Was she in love with Middleton?

Middleton hadn't come to apologize, after all. Perhaps Elizabeth had dissuaded him.

He recalled everything that Elizabeth had said, and her anxiety that he should see Middleton before the Redcoat leader was told who Rollison was. She had assured him that Middleton was on the way. There was no reason at all why she should have dissuaded him, so there was an obvious question :

Why hadn't Middleton turned up?

Rollison stood up abruptly, went to the door, hesitated, then switched out the light and stepped on to the path. He heard a youth singing, some way off; heard footsteps as late birds went to their chalets.

He closed his door, and stood still, listening for any nearer sounds. He heard none.

He knew where Middleton's chalet was, and hurried towards it. Now and again he stopped, to make sure that he wasn't followed.

When he was near Middleton's chalet, he began to think that someone might be behind him. He went more cautiously. Yes, there were footsteps, stealthy but unmistakable. It was very dark, except close to the chalets; and there were dark patches of shadow, patches of blackness, where a man—a dozen men—could hide. One had failed to harm him; next time several might try.

He was within a few doors of Middleton's chalet when a man came away from it, although no door opened and there was no light. The man appeared briefly, a silhouette against a light some way off. There was no mistaking the rounded shoulders of Uncle Pi.

He disappeared.

Rollison started moving again.

The footsteps behind him also started afresh.

CHAPTER VIII

THREAT

It was quiet; dark, eerie.

The footsteps might almost have been the echoes of Rollison's own, except that he knew that they were not.

He gripped his weapon and peered about him, could make out the shape of the chalets against the dark sky; clouds had blown up, and it was much cooler. He could just discern the waving tops of bushes, and could hear them rustling.

A man walked briskly along a path near by; then a chalet door slammed, and there was silence.

Had he imagined the shadower?

Rollison turned to the door of Middleton's chalet, and tapped softly. There was no answer, and there was no light on inside. Two or three chalets in this line had lights on, but most were in darkness.

He tapped again; and still there was no answer.

Five minutes in Middleton's chalet might tell him a lot; but above everything else there was that feeling, almost a premonition, that Middleton had disappeared, like the others.

Rollison tapped for a third time, got no answer, and then walked briskly away, as if he'd given up trying. And now *was* followed. This time there was no doubt, no attempt on the part of his follower to hide the fact that he was behind.

Rollison stopped at a corner, rubber hose in hand.

A light attached to the corner chalet was not bright; yet he could be seen against it by the man who came towards him. Just one man, who drew nearer.

He became a shape—tall, dark, wearing a trilby hat. He showed up against lighted windows—and blotted some out as he passed. He wore rubber soles, and made little sound; it was familiar, almost frightening.

Rollison stood quite still.

The man drew within a few feet of him; and still came on. Eerie was just one word. It was almost as if the man could not see him; as if he were being followed by a ghost.

The man stopped.

He said: "I've got a gun."

It was Cy Beck.

He had a flat voice, and indistinct; not the kind of voice that it would be easy to recognize again. He spoke through a muffler or a scarf, wound about his face, and covering his mouth loosely. The light fell on his eyes; that was all Rollison could see of the face itself, but he was sure it was Beck.

"Really?" Rollison said. "Mind it doesn't go off pop, Cy. I'm a nervous man by nature."

"You're in the way," Beck said.

"It's even been suggested before," Rollison murmured, "it's almost a hardy annual. Whose way?"

"Mine."

"If I were in a more receptive mood, I might apologize," murmured Rollison, "but I'm still annoyed by the fracas in the Viennese Bar. What——"

"Rollison," said Beck, "you talk too much. I've got a gun. I wouldn't mind using it. You're in the way here—get out. Never mind why you came, never mind about those Redcoats. Just get out."

"But where's my inducement?" Rollison asked practically. "You can't expect a man just to fold up because you breathe hot air on him."

It was not so easy to be flippant. Beck was just out of reach of a blow, and probably had a gun. All this was at one with Rollison's fear for Susan Dell; he believed that Beck was quite capable of shooting, and a length of rubber hose was little use against a gun.

The night was quiet; a light went out, leaving only one, some distance off, as well as the corner light above his head.

"You can pack up and leave in the morning," Beck said. "Don't stay any longer."

Rollison didn't speak.

The man went on: "They're alive—they needn't stay that way. I could cut their throats."

Nothing in his tone suggested that he was talking for the sake of talking; he sounded more menacing because there was no expression, no emphasis; just the plain statement. "I could cut their throats," he said, calmly; and in Rollison's eyes there appeared a picture of Redcoats with red throats.

"As easily as I could shoot you," the man added.

He moved his right arm.

Rollison felt a wave of panic, and flung himself to one side. He heard a hissing sound. He felt angry with himself as he steadied, because there was no report of a shot, nothing to suggest that——

He felt a stinging pain in his eyes, and knew at once what it was: ammonia gas. Tears flooded his eyes, the lights blurred, the night went darker; but there was nothing he could do to help himself. He stretched out his hand and touched the corner of a chalet. The air was clearer here, he had taken a shot of the stuff right in his face. His eyes stung, his nose and throat burned.

He stood quite still, dabbing at his eyes, breathing in the clear air.

He was at the other man's mercy, yet felt sure that the man had gone. This was simply a warning. He didn't like the other's confidence, his quick anticipation of the way he was likely to dodge from that "shot". But it was obvious that Beck would like to avoid trouble by driving him away.

He did not know how long he stood there, but at last he felt better. He could breathe without the cool air seeming to burn his nostrils. He moved about, slowly, cautiously.

He moved, slowly. There was only the silence—broken suddenly, a long way off, by an outburst of laughter and then, clear, a woman's voice:

"*Be quiet, Tim!*"

A door banged.

That was all; Rollison was left with the quiet night and the stinging memory of the gas and of the tall man with the covered face and the flat voice and creeping menace. It had been Beck—surely? The man had said that the three Red-coats were alive but that he could cut their throats.

From the moment he had seen the fear in Susan Dell's eyes, this case had become different; deadly. The tall man had made it worse; venomous.

There wasn't much time to lose.

Middleton's chalet was only a few yards away.

If Middleton knew anything, he must be made to talk. He hadn't answered the tapping, might have been dead asleep.

Rollison moved slowly towards Middleton's chalet. He heard only his own footsteps, yet listened, ears strained, in case others were behind him.

He heard none.

He reached the door, paused, and listened; and heard nothing. He tapped, softly; and there was no response. He tapped more loudly; there was still no answer.

He turned and faced the empty lawn, the opposite line of chalets. All were in darkness, now, and he heard no sound except the faint rustling of the wind through trees and bushes, and murmuring along the grass. It was colder; much colder. He shivered.

He turned back to the door.

He didn't tap again, but took his knife from a pocket. It had many blades. Such a knife would have pleased any schoolboy, delighted any crook, and made any policeman from a flatfoot upwards the most suspicious man in the world. Among the blades were the pick-lock, a metal saw, a cold chisel; and also, a mica blade, for opening Yale locks like those on the chalets.

Convinced that he was no longer being watched, Rollison started work. Yet with his back turned to the other chalets and the grass and the dark sky, the feeling of being watched was much stronger than ever.

The lock clicked back.

He pushed the door open, and it squeaked; there was no other sound.

Why wasn't Middleton in his chalet?

c

Rollison closed the door and leaned against it, then shone a pencil torch round the walls. The beam fell on a large photograph—of Elizabeth Cherrell.

There she was, with all her beauty; smiling radiantly; and her photograph was by the side of Middleton's bed. What else would he find here?

The beam of the torch lowered.

It fell on Middleton, who lay on the bed, fully dressed, with a stocking tied tightly round his throat.

.   .   .   .   .

Rollison switched on the chalet light, and swept forward, knife in his hand again, the cutting blade open before he reached the Redcoat leader's side.

Middleton's eyes were closed, his lips were parted slightly; his face looked very pale, his lips, nose, and ears were blue-ish grey. The stocking was tied with cruel tightness. Rollison could not get a finger between it and his neck. Middleton seemed not to be breathing, was like a corpse. But his hands and face were warm.

Rollison slid the cutting blade between his neck and the stocking, and began to cut the nylon with slow, sawing movements; twice he nicked the skin, and blood began to flow.

Middleton didn't move; nothing suggested that there was any life left in him.

It became easier to cut.

The stocking fell apart.

There were deep ridges in Middleton's neck—ugly, red marks and swollen veins. Rollison saw these as he put the knife on the dressing-chest, then turned Middleton over on his back. His movements were swift, decisive. He pulled the single bed away from the wall, knelt beside the limp body, and began artificial respiration. It was too early to tell whether there was any hope at all for Middleton. The continual movement was exhausting; Rollison knew that he would need help if it had to be kept up too long.

He went on.

The eerie encounter with Beck—had it been Beck?—oppressed him. But he thought of Middleton's manner, Elizabeth Cherrell's anger, and Uncle Pi's disappearing figure. Uncle Pi had gone from this doorway, and Beck—call him Beck—had been near; either or both could have done this thing.

Where was Elizabeth?

Why hadn't he brought Jolly with him?

How long dare he handle this by himself?

Rollison could see Middleton's profile; a good one. In his way, Middleton was a handsome chap. His face was moving because of Rollison's pressure. Was there a little more colour in his cheeks? Was there a suggestion of movement at his lips? At his eyes?

Rollison quickened to the hope.

He began to sweat; next, to feel sweat running down his forehead, down his neck, round his waist. It had seemed cooler outside, but was hot in here. His muscles began to flag. He would not be able to keep this up much longer; he would have to go for help. There was a First Aid station at the camp, and night nurses; but why spread news of this? Jolly could——

Who had attacked Middleton?

Where was Elizabeth?

Why had Middleton been attacked?

Whose stocking was it?

Rollison felt that he couldn't go on. He knelt there, supporting himself with his hands on the sides of the bed, and looking down. His vision was blurred with sweat which had run into his eyes. Middleton's face was there in vague outline.

Then he saw Middleton's lips move, his eyes flicker.

Excitement surged through Rollison, hope that he could save the man drove exhaustion away.

CHAPTER IX

FRIGHTENED GIRL

ROLLISON sat on the chair against the wall, looking at Middleton, who was on his back on the bed; almost comatose but alive. He was breathing regularly. Rollison had piled all the clothes he could find on to the bed—two suits, as well as blankets, an overcoat, and, on top of the pile, Middleton's red coat. These covered the man, and hid the ugly red weals at the neck.

The nylon stocking lay across Rollison's right knee.

He felt rested and relaxed. Nothing took so much physical energy as keeping up artificial respiration for a long time; but there was the deep satisfaction of this reward.

He lit a cigarette, stood up, and began to search the room. He found nothing which indicated that Middleton was involved in any crime; nothing which justified questioning the man about the missing Redcoats.

Why had he been attacked?

Whose stocking was it? Had Uncle Pi been in here?

Rollison stopped searching, reminded himself that he hadn't yet been through Middleton's pockets. He went through one after the other, putting the clothes back on the man, to keep him warm. In a wallet in the red coat there was a postcard picture of Elizabeth Cherrell; and a snapshot of the two of them together, at some beach, with a background of sea and rocks.

There was some money; several pound notes and, folded and tucked away, two $100.00 bills.

.   .   .   .   .

So there was some kind of link between the Redcoat and Cy Beck.

.   .   .   .   .

Rollison went out.

A few spots of rain fell on his face before he turned and

closed the door. He had the key in his pocket. He hurried towards his own chalet, glancing round every now and again; no one appeared to be following. Two minutes after reaching the chalet, he had Jolly wide awake and struggling into his clothes.

In ten, Jolly was entering Middleton's chalet.

"Just watch, and if he comes round before I get back, come and get me—I'll be at Miss Cherrell's chalet."

"Very good, sir." Jolly's gaiety had gone, and he still had the bemused look of a man woken from a deep sleep. "Be careful, won't you?"

"Yes," Rollison said, and had never meant it more.

He went out. It was raining quite heavily now, and he shivered again. He knew where Elizabeth's chalet was—two minutes' walk away. All the chalets except one were in darkness; and as he passed that, he heard a child whimpering.

Six thousand Campers and fifteen hundred workers were sleeping here; and an attempt had been made to kill Middleton. He kept that well in front of his mind—attempted murder, and all that it meant. There was the shadowy figure of the tall man, almost certainly Beck, with the tell-tale flat voice and the menace and the talk of murder—and a pistol which could spray ammonia gas.

Rollison could still feel the soreness at his mouth and nose, and his eyes felt as if a gust of wind had blown sand into them. All that had been forgotten in the emergency.

He reached Elizabeth's chalet; like the others, it was in darkness. He forced the lock, hearing little sound until he stepped inside. The door didn't squeak; after a few seconds he could hear the girl's even breathing.

He shone his pencil torch.

The beam fell on Elizabeth, and she stirred. He moved the light quickly. She was lying on her back, looking quite normal; sleeping beauty. He closed the door, then began to search the chalet, his torch his only light.

He found a photograph of Middleton.

He found no dollar bills.

He heard a stirring of movement, and turned to look at

the girl. He sensed that she had woken up, then heard her sharp intake of breath. He moved the torch again. The light shone on her eyes, and she closed them against the glare. He backed away, standing by the door. Her breathing was fierce and agitated, but she didn't cry out.

At last Rollison switched on the light.

She was sitting up in bed. She wore a flimsy nightdress, white and frilly at the shallow V of the neck. In spite of the fear in her eyes, her beauty shone through, hardly real. She hadn't known who he was, until now; he saw the shock of recognition. She leaned back on her pillows, staring, her lips parted. Her hair was an untidy halo.

"Hallo, Liz," he said. "Sleeping nicely?"

She didn't answer.

He moved towards her. He felt that he had to find out, *now*, whether she knew anything about the strangling, and he might be able to frighten her into a confession. She didn't cringe away, just stared fixedly. He picked up a stocking, one stocking, which lay over the foot of the bed. It looked the same shade as the strangler-stocking, which was now in his pocket; and as sheer and soft. He ran this over his hands, gently, and she watched. She hadn't yet spoken, but she had recovered from the first shock.

"Where's the other one?" he asked.

"Oth—other—what?" He could only just hear her voice.

"Stocking."

"It's—there."

"Sure?"

She looked towards the end of the bed. There was a brassière; a pair of panties; a slip; that was all.

"It must—have fallen."

"Think so?" he asked. He held the stocking in front of him, stretched between his two hands, and went slowly towards her. She didn't cringe away, but moved back defensively. Her gaze was on his eyes at first, and then on the stocking. He drew very close to her, then stopped, with the stocking stretched out above her head.

"What——" she began, and couldn't get another word out.

Rollison lowered the stocking behind her, until it touched the pillow; then he pulled it against the back of her neck, crossed it, and twisted. She snatched at it. Terror filled her eyes—those eyes which were so beautiful. She plucked at it, although for a moment he held it tightly and she could hardly breathe.

She didn't *scream*.

He held it tight.

"What do you think *he* felt? That's how you did it, isn't it? That's how you killed him, how——"

He let the stocking relax. Elizabeth's hands went to her neck and she fingered the flesh, but she didn't speak, just looked at him with her great eyes. She was breathing heavily; gaspingly.

"Let's have the truth, Liz," he said. "You killed him. Why?"

"I don't—I don't know what you're talking about."

"Why did you kill him?"

"I didn't kill anybody!"

"Your stocking was round his neck." Rollison took the strangler-stocking from his pocket; it was in two pieces. He took the other from Elizabeth's neck, and laid it on the bed, then put the two pieces of the other stocking together. They looked identical in colour, gauge, and size. He felt sure that they made a pair.

"See," he said. "Yours."

"I don't know what you're talking about," she repeated. She was still breathing hard, but was calmer; he admired the way she fought against panic, and kept her head. "Who am I supposed to have killed? Who——"

"Middleton."

Her whole face changed; horror, dread, shock sprang into her eyes, her body seemed to go stiff. Until then she hadn't been able to understand what he was doing, she had been puzzled; or she might have been trying to convince him that she was. Now he had no doubt that he saw her true reaction —she could not pretend about this.

"*No!*" she cried.

She flung back the bedclothes. Her legs were golden, lovely. She slid them out of bed to the floor, and stood up. The nylon nightdress was a sheath for a figure of beauty which could take his mind off thought of murder and violence—could compel him to look only at her.

"It isn't true," she said, in a hoarse, broken voice. In a moment she was by Rollison, holding his hands, gripping them tightly, fiercely. "Dick's not dead, you're frightening me, Dick's not——"

She caught her breath.

He flashed: "Why should I try to frighten you?"

"*He's not dead!*"

"What's he been doing, why should anyone want him dead?"

"*He's not dead!*" She snatched one hand away, and struck at Rollison's face. "He's not, you're lying, he can't, he——"

She struck him again, then took him off guard by thrusting him vigorously to one side. He staggered, caught his foot on a shoe, and fell against the wall.

Elizabeth reached the door.

"Liz——"

She opened it. Wind howled in, blowing her flimsy nightdress against her body, making it billow out behind. She was barefoot, bareheaded. She rushed into the night, and before Rollison could reach the door, she was running along the path. He snatched up the torch and ran after her. A light went on at a chalet. He could hear the pattering of Elizabeth's feet and her breathing as it floated back to him. The lights at the corner chalets showed her white, ghostly figure as she raced across a lawn towards Middleton's chalet line.

Rollison caught up with her.

"Liz——"

She shot out a hand, to strike him. He grabbed her arm.

"*Let me go!*"

"Liz——"

She pulled herself free.

The rain was hissing down and the wind was blowing,

and her nightdress was moulded to her. He gripped her round the shoulders, and her body struck cold through the nylon; cold but soft.

"Liz, listen to me, don't——"

She tried to free herself, but could not. Then Rollison heard someone else coming, across the lawn with swift, light footsteps. Still holding her, he turned round. He saw a man dressed in something pale; pyjamas? He didn't recognize him.

Liz wrenched herself free.

The man leapt at Rollison. He was much smaller than the big man who had pretended to be drunk. He cracked a fist on Rollison's jaw, but wasn't much of a boxer, and lost his balance. Rollison hit him, saw him fall back, and turned and raced after Liz. She was very near Middleton's chalet, where the light was on. There wasn't a hope of catching her until she reached it.

The rain beat down.

Rollison saw her disappear, and immediately heard the din as she beat upon the door of Middleton's chalet. He could imagine Jolly, startled. He ran on through the rain, slipping on the cement path. He glanced round, but didn't see the man who had attacked him. He reached the chalet as Jolly opened the door and the light streamed upon the girl.

She looked like marble.

"All right, Jolly," Rollison said.

Jolly stood aside.

"Tell anyone who comes out that it's all right."

Jolly went out.

The girl rushed into the chalet. Rollison couldn't see her face, but hardly needed to. She flung herself on her knees by Middleton's side. She gripped his shoulders, and began to talk to him in a wild, hysterical voice.

"Dick, you're not dead, tell me you're not dead. Dick, Dick, wake up! You're not dead, I don't believe you're dead, Dick——"

Middleton opened his eyes.

It was probably the first time he had come round. He

looked blankly at Elizabeth, couldn't have had any idea what this was all about. Then Elizabeth moved her head forward, and hid her bewilderment from Rollison. She began to cry.

She was still crying, but less wildly, when Rollison drew her away. Middleton looked dazed, but watched her. There was a moment of quiet, the first since she had reached here.

"I'll take her back to her chalet," Rollison said quietly. "Middleton, I'll see you soon. Keep warm." Rollison looked at Elizabeth, then suddenly put an arm beneath her shoulders and another beneath her knees, and lifted her.

Jolly appeared, and said something that sounded like : "All's well, sir."

Rollison stepped out into the rain. A fierce squall struck at him. He was going into the wind, and Elizabeth was lovely but not a light weight. He hurried, but couldn't run. It wasn't far. Elizabeth was wet through; she needed a hot bath or a shower, a brisk rub down.

They reached her chalet.

Uncle Pi, in a dressing-gown, hair wet and dishevelled, stood just inside.

CHAPTER X

UNCLE PI

"Just put her in that chair," Uncle Pi said, "and then put a blanket round her. I'll get a couple of the girls to lend a hand." His voice was clipped; he gave an impression of fighting back his rage.

His brown eyes usually had a soft, a gentle light. They changed as he looked at Elizabeth, and in that moment Rollison knew that he was in love with the girl. It was only for a moment; then Rollison put Elizabeth on to the chair, and Uncle Pi went out.

Rollison heard a tap at a nearby door, as he put a blanket round Elizabeth's shoulders. She had started to shiver, and couldn't control it. Rollison knew that nothing would help until she was warm again.

He heard voices.

Uncle Pi came back. He glanced at Elizabeth with familiar gentleness in his eyes, and then at Rollison. His gaze hardened; it was easy to believe that Uncle Pi could hate.

He said : "They'll be here in a jiffy."

"Good."

"Pi," a girl called out, "why don't you take her across to the baths?"

"Good idea," Uncle Pi said.

He moved towards Elizabeth. He looked down at her; she was shivering violently, and her eyes were closed.

"I'll take her," Rollison said.

"I'll lead the way." Whatever Uncle Pi was thinking, he kept himself under stern control.

The blanket was already damp from her body, so Rollison did not take it away. Light shone out from a chalet two doors removed; and there was another light above a doorway marked *Lasses* on the other side of the lawn which ran between the chalet lines. Rollison took Elizabeth across, and inside. Uncle Pi followed. There were rows of showers and ordinary baths.

"Better fill a bath," Rollison said.

"Here we are," a girl called, and came hurrying, "you two had better get out, or there'll be a scandal."

She was short and plump, and had frizzy hair in a net. The girl with her was tall and on the lean side. Rollison had seen neither of them before. They bustled him and Uncle Pi out. Water was splashing into the bath before the men left the building.

The plump girl came hurrying.

"We'll put her in my bed. Have it ready, Pi."

"Right."

The two men walked across the lawn together. Lights were at other windows, two doors were open, someone called out in a muted voice.

"It's all right," Uncle Pi called. "Forget it." He looked round at Rollison. "Wait for me at Liz's chalet, will you?"

He went into another, and Rollison saw him bending over the bed. Two men came along to speak to the Pied Piper, and he satisfied them.

Rollison, soaked to the skin, would leave tell-tale signs if he searched again. So he struggled to light a cigarette, and succeeded as Uncle Pi came in.

The brown eyes were cold and hostile.

"I don't care who you are," he said very carefully. "I don't care if you're the best detective in England, Europe, or the whole damned world, but keep your hands off Liz. Understand?"

Rollison said : "Listen, Wray, she——"

"Just keep your hands off Liz," Uncle Pi went on. "She can't have anything to do with—whatever you're here to do. *She* doesn't know a thing about the fellows who've disappeared, if that's what you're after. Just leave her alone—understand?"

Rollison said : "I found Middleton, nearly dead."

The brown eyes didn't soften.

"Strangled," Rollison said.

"If you think——"

"With her stocking."

"That's not true."

"Listen," Rollison said patiently, "get mad at me, get mad at the whole world if you must, but don't lose your sense of proportion. I tell you that Middleton was nearly strangled with Liz's stocking. If I'd been ten minutes later, he would probably have died. I thought she might know something about it. I tried to panic her into admitting it."

"You panicked her," Uncle Pi sneered. "You frightened the wits out of her. I could——" He had his hands clenched by his side; he didn't raise them. "You must be crazy," he went on, "to think that she would——" He broke off.

"It was her stocking," Rollison insisted.

"She's so much in love with him that——" Uncle Pi began, only to break off again. He seemed to relax. He went to the dressing-chest and helped himself from a packet of cigarettes which Rollison hadn't noticed; and to a match. He put both boxes down. "I hope you're satisfied that she didn't do it, now."

"I think so," Rollison said, "but there are other things I have to satisfy myself about. What's worrying Middleton?"

"I don't know any more than you."

"Pi," Rollison said, and took a cigarette from the packet, lit it, and flicked the match out of the doorway, "a girl Camper disappeared tonight. That makes four disappearances. Something very crooked is going on here. Middleton could be in it. I think Liz is frightened in case he is—perhaps because she knows he is. If he's a crook——"

Uncle Pi gave a twisted smile. His eyes had lost their cold hostility, but hadn't their true glow.

"You can talk! If Dick Middleton's a crook, he's not the man for Liz. But I'm supposed to buy that one, and praise you for trying to prove that he's a crook by terrifying her. I can't and won't. When I saw you running after her, I could have——" He broke off.

"Killed," Rollison murmured.

"Sticks and stones may break my bones," quoth Uncle Pi,

with a smile which made him seem nearer his normal self, "but names will never hurt me! If I'd split your skull I couldn't have cared less. Still, perhaps it's as well I didn't."

Rollison grinned.

"Thanks! Been to Middleton's chalet tonight?"

Uncle Pi could deny that he had. If he did, then it would suggest a guilty conscience; at least, an urgent need for secrecy. Instead, he gave his slow, amused smile.

"Suspecting me?"

"Could be."

"What time?"

"Say an hour ago—or less." Rollison was very casual.

Uncle Pi said slowly: "Yes. I went to Middleton's chalet. I didn't go in. I didn't hear a sound." His eyes seemed to glow with gentle defiance. "Do I hear one across the way?" he asked.

They looked across at *Lasses,* and the plump girl was standing and beckoning them and making little cooing noises, to try to attract their attention without disturbing anyone else.

They looked across at *Lasses,* and the plump girl was like dashes of yellow in the light from the baths. Elizabeth was sitting on a stool, away from the door. She was fully awake, and no longer trembling. The girls had fetched her dressing-gown and put it on her, and she wore slippers.

"I can walk," she said.

"Walk to me," said Rollison.

He lifted her with little effort, and carried her across the lawn at the double. Soon he put her on the bed. The tall girl and the plump one began to shoo him out.

"Just a minute," Rollison protested.

"Rollison——" began Uncle Pi.

"I said, *out,*" said the lean girl, firmly.

Rollison grinned at her, slid his arm round her waist and squeezed; and she gasped. He held the plump girl, too, and stood by the door, an arm round each. Elizabeth lay on the bed, cheeks flushed, eyes very bright—as if she were amused in spite of herself.

"Liz," Rollison said, "what's it all about? What makes you think they'll kill Dick Middleton?"

She closed her eyes.

"Now this really *is* enough," said the lean girl, and pulled herself free. "Get out, or I'll send for the Security boys."

She pushed Rollison and Uncle Pi towards the door.

The rain beat down on them, and another gust smashed upon the chalets, rattling windows and doors, sending a metal chair crashing over with noise enough to waken the whole chalet line. Wet through, they hurried to Uncle Pi's chalet.

"I won't come in," Rollison said.

"Stand in the rain, then, but you'll listen to me. What makes you think that Liz believes that someone might want to murder Dick?"

"It's one of the things I had to find out," Rollison said quietly. "Is she terrified for him? I think yes. She believes, she *knows* that he's in danger. I wish I could be sure that she isn't."

"Where's the danger?"

"Jealous rival, perhaps," Rollison said lightly.

"Like me."

"Like you."

"Evidence?" murmured Uncle Pi.

"Very vague."

"Let's know if it gets any clearer," said Uncle Pi. "I didn't go into Dick's chalet. I——" He broke off. "Why the devil should I tell you what I was doing, anyway?"

"Please yourself," Rollison said, abruptly.

He turned and walked off.

He half-expected Uncle Pi to follow him, but the hunchback didn't; as far as Rollison could tell, he did not watch, just let him walk off without showing any further sign of curiosity.

He had been watching Elizabeth's chalet; or at least, alert for trouble. He might have been expecting it.

Someone had nearly murdered Middleton, using Liz's stocking.

Did the two men hate each other because of Liz? Was that why Liz behaved so oddly? Judging from the frenzy, she was in love with Middleton, so Uncle Pi had the greater cause for jealousy. Gentle, soothing, well-loved Uncle Pi—who could hit very hard.

There was Middleton, whose wife had walked out on him according to general belief; in love; and with Liz in love with him; and with two $100.00 notes in his wallet.

The wife might have cause to hate, too. It was time to find her.

. . . . . .

Jolly was still patiently on duty. Middleton was sitting up on the pillows, with two coats round him, smoking. He looked much better, the greyness had gone. Uncle Pi, who ought to have been worried about him, obviously wasn't.

"Rollison," he said at once, "what's all this about?"

"Don't you know?"

"How the hell should I?" demanded Middleton. His voice was hoarse and seemed to hurt him. "I was coming to see you. I was going—going to say that I was sorry I blew my top this evening. *You* weren't the drunk. Then someone threw a sack or a cloth over my head, and I felt that damned thing tightening round my neck." He shuddered. "I shan't forget it in a hurry."

"What time was this?"

"Elevenish, I suppose."

"Where?"

"Just outside here."

"And then—black out?"

"Yes." Middleton took the cigarette from his lips. "What was Liz doing here, why did she behave like that?"

"She thought you were dead," Rollison said grimly. "You ought to have been, with that stocking tied round your neck for so long." He didn't tell Middleton that it was Liz's stocking. "Feel all right now?"

"I don't exactly want to get up and push a bus over, but I'm all right."

He could be badly shaken now. Mention of $100.00 bills might do it, but that would betray too much. Accusing Liz might, too; but wasn't likely. But Middleton had to be shaken into talking.

"Of course we'll have to tell the police," Rollison said.

"Don't be a fool!" snapped Middleton. The idea frightened him, exactly as Rollison hoped it would. Then he collected his wits. "If you fetch the police here and the story gets round that there's been an attempted murder, there'll be panic in the place. You ask Aird, and see what *he* says." He leaned forward and stubbed out his cigarette. "Besides, I'm told you're the man to find out what's happening around here."

That was almost a sneer.

Rollison put his head on one side, as he studied the man.

"Who told you?"

"I met Llewellyn. If I hadn't, I'd have come to tell you I was prepared to apologize."

That sounded characteristic.

"Forget it," Rollison said, and went on in the same voice : "Is your wife on the Camp, Middleton?"

Middleton coloured furiously, taken completely by surprise.

"Good—good lord, no !"

"Does she hate you?"

"Hate——" began Middleton, and then grinned; and the grin became a laugh. It wasn't normal, but had the metallic note of hysteria.

Rollison watched him, stonily. He recovered, but his eyes were bright, his cheeks flushed. Shock?

"Think he needs a doctor?" Rollison asked the silent Jolly.

"I don't want anyone fussing over me," growled Middleton. "I'm all right."

Rollison shrugged, and went out.

Jolly followed him, and closed the door.

"We could wait and see what happens next," Rollison

said, "and whether there'll be another attack on him. We could also go and do some thinking."

He began to walk towards his own chalet line, with Jolly almost trotting beside him; and they trod on soaking wet grass, here and there in a pool of water, while the rain beat down on them. He told Jolly all that had happened, briefly. Jolly kept his own counsel, probably because his feet were wet and he felt miserable.

"What are your major impressions, Jolly?"

"Middleton's peculiar laughter." Jolly proved that he had been thinking. "And——" He shrugged. "Perhaps the fact that he didn't die."

"You've got something there," Rollison agreed. "Add the shock—almost hysterical amusement—at the idea that his wife might be here and vengeful. Have we his home address?"

"No, sir, but I can get it first thing in the morning."

"Good. Do. And we need help that we know we can rely on—say Bill Ebbutt and two or three of his boys. For once in your life you'll have to be glad to see our prize-fighter."

"I took the precaution, sir, of telephoning Mr. Ebbutt earlier in the evening and telling him that I thought it likely that you would try to find something for him to do here," Jolly said suavely. "He assured me that he would be *very* happy to come."

Rollison eyed him up and down. He was wet and be-draggled; his sparse hair was plastered down; it would not be long before he began to shiver. He was just—Jolly.

"So you did, and he did," Rollison said. "I ought to dis-solve partnership." And felt suddenly light-hearted. "Go and get a hot shower and turn in."

"After you, sir," Jolly said meekly.

"We'll go together," Rollison decided. "Let's get our rain-coats."

He moved.

He was the first to see the drawing on the dressing-chest. It was on a sheet of note-paper, with lines on it—just a crude crayon drawing, such as a child might scrawl. But no child had drawn this. There were three men, one lying down, the others sitting. Each wore a red coat. At the throat of each was a red gash.

He could almost hear that flat voice : "I could cut their throats." He could almost see Susan Dell. He had seen her in the flesh only twice, yet she was as vivid to him as Elizabeth.

He could almost see the tall, shadowy figure of the man who had squirted ammonia gas at him.

"You were wrong, Jolly," he said, slowly. "You shouldn't have telephoned to warn Bill, you should have told him to come at once. I wonder how many tall, thin men there are at the Camp."

"Why, sir?"

"Each one's suspect," Rollison said. "Say fifty. A hundred?" He looked at the drawing again. "Jolly, we've a lot to do, and not much time to do it in. At least we've a lead, with Cy Beck."

.   .   .   .

Some time earlier, Beck had left a coffee bar and walked slowly through the rain towards his own chalet. A woman—his wife—lay on the bed in the far corner, with the bed-clothes up to her shoulders. She snatched one hand out and covered her eyes as Beck switched on the light.

He closed the door.

"You might *warn* me," the woman said. "It's getting cold, isn't it?"

"It's getting warm," Cy said. "That damned Rollison's come just at the wrong time." He lit a cigarette, and stood staring down at his wife as he unwound the scarf, tossed the hat to a chair, and took a little pistol, which looked like a toy, from his pocket. "We want another three days."

"That's what you said last night !"

"That's right," said Cy. He looked painfully thin, his cheeks were sunken, his eyes were dark and glowed almost with a feverish light. "I still want three. We had to lose Clark, didn't we? Not that it would have mattered, as things turned out. I've told Rollison to leave the Camp. He'd better go."

His wife sat up. She was easy to look at; a handsome blonde. "Cy, you're crazy, Rollison can't be frightened off."

"Can't he?" Cy rubbed the side of his neck. "Well, he can be fooled. Perhaps you're the one to fool him. We've got to get him looking in the wrong place, until we've finished. Rather than lose, I'd——"

He looked vicious; savage.

"Don't look like that," his wife said, "you make me shiver. I don't care what you say, it's getting *cold*."

CHAPTER XI

TOP O' THE MORNING

"Good morning, sir," said Jolly. "And a beautiful morning it is."

Rollison opened one eye.

This showed him Jolly in a light-grey suit and a beaming smile, even a light in his eyes. It showed him the window with sunlight shining through. Apart from that, it revealed the chalet as it had been when he had returned from the hot bath; and also the crude drawing which had been left for his edification.

He struggled up.

Jolly was pouring tea from a thermos flask.

"I'm sorry that it isn't possible to obtain a pot of tea," he said, almost gaily, "but the Mirror Bar supplies these vacuum flasks for those who like a little extra comfort. I hope it is to your liking, sir."

"Thanks." Rollison took a cup cautiously.

"The newspapers, sir," said Jolly, pulling these from his coat pocket and handing them to Rollison with a flourish. "I am happy to say that there is nothing particularly dismal or depressing in them."

"Jolly," said Rollison, "what's happened to you?"

"To me, sir? In what way?"

"We're at Butlin's, remember. You were going to hate every minute of it."

"Indeed, sir," murmured Jolly. "I imagine that it must be the holiday atmosphere of the establishment, I can't think of anything else. Is there any more you require, sir, or shall I run your bath?"

"I'll run my own bath," Rollison said. "I can't stand you in this mood."

"*Very* good, sir. Oh, I took the liberty of telephoning Mr. Ebbutt, knowing that he is always up and about at six o'clock. He was already having a work-out in the gymnasium. I explained a little more precisely, and with three of his friends he will start out at nine o'clock this morning. He estimates that the journey will take eight or nine hours, so by this evening we shall have reinforcements."

He rubbed his hands, as if gleefully.

"Yes," said Rollison. "Thanks. Nothing else?"

"Nothing of any significance," Jolly told him blandly. "On the way to fetch the tea I saw Uncle Pi, by himself except for several small children. Mr. Middleton appears to have slept well."

"Eh?"

"So he informs me, sir, I called on him at eight-fifteen. A few minutes afterwards, Miss Cherrell was still asleep. Everything else in the Camp seems quite normal, sir, I——"

He stopped; he winced—slightly.

"*Good morning, Campers,*" came the voice over the Camp radio, "*and what a beautiful morning it is! The bad weather blew itself out during the night, and now we're ready for another perfect day's fun and games, and we mean fun and games. Breakfast will be served from nine o'clock, that is in exactly half an hour. Here are some of the morning's events—choose whichever you like, and remember that they are timed so that you can take part in as many as possible. From ten until ten-thirty there will be games on the playing-field, then for cyclists there is the Mystery Bike Hike, and again on the playing-field, the model aeroplane competitions. For dancing enthusiasts, lessons . . .*"

Rollison sipped his tea.

Jolly waited, resignedly.

Words floated into Rollison's consciousness; words like Tombola, Square Dancing, Auditions, cricket, children. Weather conditions, the Camp was assured, were perfect for flying; Campers were exhorted to see the Camp from the air; and also to see the Welsh Coast.

He grinned.

"Putting first things first," he said. "All right, Jolly, off you go."

"I've Middleton's home address here, sir." Jolly handed Rollison a slip of paper. "And I hope to get the information about any others who were at the Camp when Clark was here before," Jolly said. "I will produce it just as quickly as possible."

"Yes. Oh, wait a minute. As Bill Ebbutt's coming down with three others, we shall want them to behave as Campers. How can we get them into the Camp? It's full up."

Jolly was seraphic.

"As a matter of fact, sir, yesterday I was fortunate enough to discover that a party due to take several chalets for a long week-end has cancelled the booking, and consequently I was able to put a word in for some—ah—friends of mine. I don't think the matter of accommodation will be very difficult."

Rollison looked at him almost in consternation.

"Good morning, sir," said Jolly, and positively frisked out.

To those who did not know him well, Jolly in this guise might not have appeared remarkable. To Rollison, whom he had served for over twenty years, it was a revelation, a phenomenon, a cataclysmic upheaval, and even a fantastic *volte face*. It was simply not Jolly's nature to display *joie de vivre*; his contentment was the contentment of the solemn face and the occasionally twinkling eye.

Rollison finished his tea, got out of bed, heard Jolly's door slam, and went into Jolly's room. He watched from Jolly's door as his man walked away briskly, shoulders squared and well back, feet planted firmly on the path, arms swinging; and a faint but distinct sound of whistling came back to Rollison—Jolly was at *La Ronde* again.

"Hum," breathed Rollison. "Who?"

His own mood was heavy.

It was not lightened by a glimpse of the drawing. That told him that someone had been able to pick the lock of this door and leave the sketch with its implicit threat.

There had been the tall, shadowy man with the ammonia-gas, who had exerted a curiously dominating influence; and who, above everything else, had been so confident and so sure of himself.

Cy Beck?

There were the disappearances.

There was the fact of Elizabeth's stocking round Middleton's neck.

There was Middleton's hysteria and the possibility of bitter rivalry for Elizabeth's hand.

Rollison was glad of the telephone specially installed for him, and put through a London call, to Superintendent Grice's flat.

Grice hadn't left for the Yard. He listened, and then said :

"I remember Clark, Rolly. We always suspected he was one of a big gang of jewel thieves, but we never found the stuff he took. We didn't know he was in any dollar racket. Cyrus Beck doesn't ring a bell, but I'll check—I've noted that description. You might have uncovered something."

"My usual luck," murmured Rollison.

"That's right ! As for this chap Middleton. I'll find out what I can. Anything else ?"

"Not yet." Rollison protested. "I've only had a day to work in, you've had weeks."

The Yard man had the grace to laugh. Feeling rather better, Rollison rang off and went across to the *Lads*. He had a cold bath, for the morning was warming up, returned to the chalet, shaved, and dressed. His brief brightness faded. Susan Dell had disappeared, Elizabeth Cherrell took some explaining; the eyes of each girl were so beautiful.

The eyes of the blonde he saw on the way to breakfast, with the music of the radio in his ears, were not beautiful. There was nothing particularly wrong with them, however. They were quite nice grey eyes, brightened by mascara put on expertly. The blonde was nicely made up and nicely turned out. She was probably in the early thirties. She did not make the mistake of overdoing make-up or under-doing her clothes. Her tennis skirt was knee length and not, like many, an abbreviated version which showed much thigh.

Anyone with eyes could see that she had quite a figure. Her white blouse, without exactly disguising this, at least did little to exaggerate her charm. She had a pleasant face, perhaps a little hard when one came to look into it, and her hair was too fair; almost brassy. But on the whole, not bad at all.

A little later, Rollison found her at his table instead of a greybeard who had mumbled over his plate.

"Why, hallo!" he said. "Good morning."

"*Good* morning." She was opposite him. "I do hope you don't mind, but I changed tables—I do like to be near the window, it gets rather warm, doesn't it?"

"Can do," he agreed. "I'm delighted."

He was gallant. He was so gallant that the youths who came along late for breakfast appeared to be spellbound by his flow of small-talk. He himself seemed to be genuinely regretful when they'd finished the meal.

Was he going to the morning-coffee dance?

"I *may* be able to get there," Rollison said. "One never knows—duty, and all that."

He beamed, saw her to the door, bowed. She didn't look back. He didn't stare after her, but was very thoughtful.

Redcoats waved.

Uncle Pi came out of a shop, hurrying, and with a preoccupied air. Nothing he did suggested that he knew that eleven small boys and seven small girls were following him. These came out of the shop in twos and threes, hurrying, gazing, worshipping. Uncle Pi caught sight of Rollison, waved, and went on. The crocodile of children followed—and grew longer. Children ran across the roads towards him, called, "Oo, there's Uncle Pi," or laid wait for him at the corners, greeted him, and then fell in behind. To each greeting, he returned a word or two which satisfied; or patted a curly head, pulled a pig-tail, or tweaked an ear.

He vanished.

His tail vanished, too.

"Wonderful, isn't it?" The speaker was Aird, who approached from a corner as Rollison turned. Aird looked smaller, more compact, and less right for the Camp than ever. He took out cigarettes. "Uncle Pi, I mean—the best Uncle we've ever had here." His eyes smiled. "Weren't you detailed to assist him?"

"I may do yet," Rollison said. He did not add that that was because Middleton had detailed the vanished Peverill to help Uncle Pi.

"How are things going?" Aird asked. "No news of Clark or the girl?" The morning seemed to have removed most of his fears. It would be interesting to see his face if he knew about a near-strangling and hysteria. "Anything news from you?"

"There were night excitements, I'll tell you about them later," Rollison said. "Had any complaints?"

"Several—that there were too many people shouting about late last night." Aird smiled again. "They came from Campers near Middleton and Miss Cherrell. Nothing serious, I hope."

He knew quite a lot; it must be hard to keep secrets here.

"As it turned out, no."

Aird said: "Like that, is it?" He looked into Rollison's eyes. "Don't let anything get out of hand, will you?"

"I don't quite follow," Rollison said.

"I've been thinking that these people have had things all their own way. If they come up against some stiff opposition, they might turn nasty. Llewellyn told me about the fight in the Viennese Bar. Be careful."

"I'm fond of life, too," Rollison smiled. "And I must hurry."

As he went off he knew that Aird was standing and watching him, thoughtfully.

Elizabeth was still asleep . . .

Middleton was no longer in his chalet . . .

Rollison went on to the ballroom in the South Camp, where the children were assembled. Outside it was bright sunlight, inside shadowy, gloomy—and fantastic. The great room was swarming with children. A few parents sat round the walls watching the mass of children laughing, shrieking, running, fighting, crying, eating, blowing up balloons, bouncing balls, laughing.

At the far end of the ballroom, where by night the band would play, were Uncle Pi and two girl Redcoats. As Rollison reached them, they were in a huddle. Uncle Pi broke it. He saw Rollison and grinned.

"Aren't they having a wonderful time? You're off duty," he said. "I've got someone else for the under-fives! Meet Aunt Alice, who's a regular, and Aunt Hilda, who's volunteered to help out instead of you."

Both girls were nice to look at; pleasant.

"Now watch this," Uncle Pi said. He tapped the microphone in front of him, to check that it was live, then began to whistle into it.

The whistling was soft and gentle, with nothing piercing or shrill about it. The amazing thing, the miracle, was the way it affected the children. The shrieking, screaming, crying, laughing tumult died away; there was a hush. Even the toddlers, down to the very youngest, stopped and gazed at Uncle Pi as he stood swaying gently, smiling, whistling.

The parents were quiet, too.

Then a man appeared at the door, a silhouette against the bright sunlight. It was Jolly.

CHAPTER XII

A MAN NAMED CYRUS

ROLLISON walked round the sides of the ballroom towards Jolly, while Uncle Pi went on whistling, and children and parents watched, enraptured. Only two or three babies in arms were fractious. As Rollison met Jolly, Uncle Pi stopped whistling. In spite of his eagerness to know what Jolly wanted, Rollison turned round.

Uncle Pi was smiling.

"Good morning, children," he said.

"*Good morning, Uncle Pi!*" came back in unison. It wasn't exactly a roar, but every child who could frame the words seemed to call out. The sound filled the great room, gave a clear indication of contentment.

Rollison forced himself to go out into the blazing sunlight. It was now very warm; there was a beading of sweat on Jolly's forehead and lips.

"Any luck, Jolly?"

"I think there might be a little, sir," Jolly said. "I was anxious to let you know as quickly as possible, I thought you might go off with the children, and it would have been difficult to find you. I have the names of two people who were at the camp at the same time as the men Clark and Beck—*and* as Susan Dell."

Rollison said softly : "*Very* nice work."

"There are two men," Jolly said. "One is no stranger, sir—a Eustace Rickett, an ex-prize-fighter, who——"

"My Viennese Bar pal?"

"Yes, sir."

"And?"

"And Mrs. Beck," Jolly said. "She's a blonde, much younger than Beck himself, quite personable."

"What's her first name?"

"Rosa."

92

"Rosa?"

"Yes, sir. I've been through the records with the help of a—ah—friend, and it is virtually certain that we now know the only people who were at the Camp during the disappearance periods."

"Your friend deserves a medal."

Jolly beamed.

"I fully agree, sir," he said. "One other thing: I've talked to the night-patrol who was on duty in Beck's chalet line last night. He didn't see Beck go out, but there was a light on in the chalet, and man and wife were talking a little while before you came for me last night. So the man who used the gas pistol could well be Beck."

"I'm longing for a chat with our Cy," murmured Rollison. "Thanks. Keep your eye on the ball."

"I will indeed," said Jolly. "Unless there is something you need now, I will return to the offices. I've found that arranging the accommodation for Bill Ebbutt and his men is a little more difficult than I expected. But it can be done, sir, it shall be done!"

"Off with you," said Rollison, faintly.

Jolly turned and positively bounded towards the railway bridge, the Middle Camp and the offices. As he disappeared over the bridge, a Camp bus stopped by Rollison's side. He jumped on, and passed Jolly near the office.

Rollison went into the main office, to watch as his man appeared. Jolly went straight towards one of the Reception clerks, and beamed.

She was the woman Jolly had been with on Rollison's arrival.

Her face lit up. It was a nice face, round, with a nose that wrinkled easily and lips which puckered and eyes which looked as if they could laugh easily. Her hair was a mass of greying curls. She was smart in black, trimmed with white.

"Incredible," said Rollison, in an almost strangled voice. "Not *Jolly*."

He felt as if he were wilting, when he turned round, and

almost banged into Middleton. Middleton had a white choker round his neck, to hide the fact that it was red and swollen. He looked tired; worn out.

"I—er—can you spare me a minute, Mr. Rollison?"

Rollison grinned. "Ryall, cappen!"

Middleton's answering smile was strained.

"Difficult to keep that up, now. I think we'll be able to talk better outside." They went out, walking towards the swimming-pool, which presented exactly the same scene as it had yesterday; if anything, more people were in the water, and more clambering up the diving boards. A big ex-Army truck pulled up with a Redcoat in it, a cheery youth who called :

"Whose for the next flight over the Camp?"

A dozen people moved forward.

Rollison and Middleton went towards a putting-course, also crowded. Rickett's wife, the woman with the big, wet mouth, watched and followed.

"I just had to say that I realize how much I owe you for last night," Middleton said abruptly. "I didn't, until your man told me——" He broke off, and fingered his neck. "What—what made you come to see me?"

"I wanted a chat."

Middleton might have asked how Rollison had got in; he didn't. He watched the road, in sight from here. Several cars passed beneath the flags of all nations which fluttered from tall poles. Middleton could not have looked more uneasy; his heart might have been fluttering as much as the flags themselves.

"Have you—have you any idea who did it?"

"I know that Liz Cherrell's stocking was used."

Middleton said : "I—I can hardly believe it. I've just come from her. She——" He closed his eyes, moved back to a wooden seat, and dropped into it. "She told me what happened. Rol—Rollison, have you any *real* reason to believe that she did it?"

Rollison murmured : "Just the stocking."

"Is that all?"

"Absolutely all. You say you were attacked outside your chalet. Was it by a man or a woman?"

"Wouldn't have been a woman, I struggled," Middleton muttered. "I suppose she could——" He broke off again. He looked up into Rollison's eyes, and his own were tormented. "Find out for me," he begged. "I——"

"It's time you told me what's worrying you," Rollison said gently. "Why you even think it possible that Liz would want to kill you?"

Middleton cried: "It *isn't* possible!"

"Listen, Dick——" Rollison began.

"Ahoy there, Dick!" A Redcoat came hurrying towards them. "Where the hell have you been? The Great White Chief wants you, and there are a dozen of us in your office—been looking for you all over the place."

"Er—sorry," Middleton said. "Not feeling so good this morning. Sorry, Rol—Ryall. Must go. See you later."

He hurried off.

Rollison watched him go. It was a pity; Middleton had a lot on his mind, and might have unloaded some of it. It would be worth trying to break him down. The certain thing was his fear; he was living on raw nerves.

Ten minutes later, Rollison walked past Beck's chalet. It had a red door and red paint work, a blue roof, red curtains at the windows. The door was ajar. Someone was moving about inside. A pair of grey woollen socks hung on a piece of string tied from a corner of the roof to a window.

Rollison watched, from the cover of some bushes.

A woman came out.

It was the brassy-haired woman of his table, carrying several fragile-looking garments. She stretched up and pegged these on to the improvised line. She had quite a figure, and nice legs. She went back into the chalet.

"Okay," she said, a few minutes later, "I'll be seeing you, Cy."

She came out.

She wore exactly the same clothes that she had at breakfast, walked gracefully, and seemed in a hurry. She disappeared. Rollison heard her speak to a cleaner coming out of a chalet.

Beck appeared at the doorway of his. It was the first good look Rollison had of him.

Beck was very tall, about the height of the man who had used the gas pistol. His jet black hair was wiry and unruly, a great mane of hair. Even from this distance, his eyes looked almost black, too. The most remarkable thing about him was his thinness. His cheeks sunk in, the bones jutting out; his jaw seemed like bone covered with tight skin. His eyes might have been little more than sockets.

He moved easily, slamming the door. His hands were bony and thin, too, his clothes seemed to flap about him.

He walked towards the playing-fields, along one of the footpaths which bisected the chalet lines. He wore rubber-soled shoes, and made little sound. It could not have been brighter sunlight; the green of the grass was vivid after the rain, the flowers were a glory of colour. A few people were playing tennis; others were playing netball, some children were running about the grass.

But about the thin Beck there was something eerie.

Rollison watched him walk towards the playing-fields. He couldn't follow without being seen, so moved in a different direction. By hurrying, he might be able to reach the spot where Beck would come out. He had to pass the two churches and the bicycle store. Two youths on a red tricycle came hurtling along the road towards him. A woman with two children clinging to her skirts swung them out of the path of the oncoming machine.

"They ought to be stopped, tearing about like that," she said angrily. "They——"

The machine changed direction, as if to avoid a girl on the other side of the road, and swung towards Rollison. It was travelling at twenty miles an hour, a crazy speed on Camp roads. The two youths were grinning, teeth showing, eyes shining. *They weren't so young.*

Rollison saw the danger, and leapt for safety.

He felt something tear at his coat, and was nearly thrown,

recovered, and kept his balance. The woman screamed. Rollison turned, to see the tricycle crash against the kerb, and turn over. One rider leapt clear, the other went under the machine. One of the children, frightened by the mother's scream, began to cry. Several people hurried up, including two Redcoats, a man and a girl.

Someone called : "Accident."

"Anyone hurt?"

"No accident," Rollison thought coldly. He dodged the crowd, and hurried to the spot where he hoped to see Beck. There were more chalets, and another dining-hall on his right. From a corner, he saw the tall, gangling figure of Beck stepping out towards a garage; there were petrol pumps, vans, and lorries with *Butlin's* painted all over them, and several jeeps.

The Camp radio was switched on.

Rollison heard snatches; the morning's programme, Camp flights, something special for the afternoon.

He reached a spot from which he could watch Beck without being seen. Beck went to the car park and got into a grey Vauxhall. He drove off, without looking right or left; without suggesting that he thought that he was being followed.

Rollison's car was too far off for to be of use.

He ran to the garage, and called to two mechanics in the repair shop.

"Is there a taxi?" he asked urgently. "Or a drive-yourself car?"

"Well, the taxis are all out," a man told him. "You could have that old Morris, but——"

Negotiations took only a few minutes, including a telephone call to Aird. People glared at Rollison because of his speed. He reached the gates, where a porter stopped him with arms outstretched, virtually at the risk of his life.

"You can't drive like *that* in the Camp ! Why you'll——"

"A grey Vauxhall just went out," Rollison said, "Which way?"

"You can't——"

D

"Which *way*." Rollison produced a pound note.

"Okay, if you're in a hurry, I'll talk to you when you come back. That way." The man didn't take the pound.

Rollison drove out.

The old car touched fifty, which was ten miles an hour too fast for the narrow, winding road. The countryside looked beautiful in the sun; there was a touch of magic about it, and the rain had freshened the trees, the hedges, and the fields.

He came within sight of Beck and the Vauxhall. It went straight on, past a signpost reading *Pwllheli*. Not far along was a huge board near the gate of a field, reading *Butlin's Airport*. The gates were open. Rollison watched the Vauxhall, which kept on the main road and, after about three miles, ran on to a wide, smooth stretch, obviously newly made.

Ten minutes after leaving the camp, Beck had parked in one of Pwllheli's narrow streets. People thronged them. Camp badges seemed to be on every other lapel. Beck's tall figure was easy to see, as easy to follow. Rollison kept him in sight without getting too close.

Beck went into two shops; Rollison noted the names of them. One was an outfitter's, the other a tobacconist's. Back in his car, the gaunt man sat at the wheel, lighting a pipe. Rollison's car was parked some distance away; Rollison couldn't see the Vauxhall when he took his own wheel, but he would see if Beck got out again.

Beck didn't, but drove back, towards the Camp. Had the jaunt been as aimless as it seemed?

Rollison kept fifty yards behind. He saw a signpost and a big green bus, which momentarily hid Beck's car. When it was past, Beck's car was much farther ahead. Rollison put his foot down, to catch up—and a car shot out of a side road in front of him. His heart made a wild leap as he jammed on his brakes. He jolted to a standstill only inches off the other car.

Two men jumped out and rushed at him.

CHAPTER XIII.

CY BECK

ROLLISON'S engine had stalled; he stabbed at the self-starter. A third man got out of the car in front and joined in the rush. This was a beating-up—where Rickett had failed, they meant to succeed.

He reversed, engine snarling.

He swung on to the far side of the road, jammed on his brakes, changed gear, and sent the car shooting forward. The men hadn't expected him to get mobile so soon. One leapt out of the way, two others were already on one side. Rollison swung the wheel towards them. Another man leapt for dear life. The third flung something; it smashed against the window and dropped into the road with a clang, the kind of noise that a piece of iron piping might make.

Rollison cleared the trio.

He kept his foot down, and wasn't surprised to see the Vauxhall drawn up in the shade of the road, half a mile along. He wasn't surprised to see Cyrus Beck sitting at the wheel smoking his pipe.

He pulled up in front of the other car.

When he went back to it, Beck was taking his pipe from his lips. His eyes weren't really black, but very dark brown; they seemed to burn. Occasionally Rollison met that rare bird, a man with the look of evil about him; this man had it. It was in the expression of his thin, colourless lips, the burning eyes, the face. A soft wind blew his mane of black hair.

Rollison said mildly : "Hallo, Cy."

Beck didn't speak.

"I don't think we're going to get along too well," Rollison persisted. "I don't like your boy friends at all."

Beck still didn't speak.

"One way of dealing with it would be to go to the police," Rollison said. "A charge of assault and battery, with you named as the instigator, would keep you busy for a little while, wouldn't it? I could fix Rickett, too. Any reasonable objections?"

Beck put his pipe to his mouth, leaned forward, and switched on the engine. He glanced away from Rollison, then back at him.

It was a moment when he could take and have a chance to keep the ascendency, which was not the Toff's idea at all.

The Toff stretched his arm out, and switched off the ignition. He beamed. Beck glowered and struck at his arm; and Rollison twisted his fingers, caught the bony wrist, and made Beck gasp.

"Real hair or a wig, that is the question," Rollison burbled, and plucked at Beck's hair.

He tugged; Beck's eyes watered with a sudden pain, but the grip on his wrist held him rigid.

Rollison said gently : "Real hair on a bad man, Cy. One of us is going to get hurt. Don't put your strong-arm men on me again. Understand?"

He pulled Beck's hair again, lightly, then let him go, beamed, and went back to his own car. He guessed at the things Beck would like to say and do; in fact, all he did was to glower, put the car into gear, and start off. There was just room for him to get past the borrowed Morris.

He didn't look back.

"Cool," mused Rollison. "He's not bad at all." He had an odd feeling, much as he had the previous night when the man with the flat voice had threatened him. Cyrus Beck was absolutely confident of himself; thought he could afford to sneer, to be insolent, to threaten. Well, he was shaken now—but it was odd that he hadn't said a word.

Rollison got back into the Morris.

When he reached the Camp gates, he felt subdued. He was further subdued by the man on duty, who had "promised" to talk to him later. He flayed Rollison with his tongue; only idiots or criminals drove at such speed in the Camp, didn't he know there were children about, did he want reporting, who the hell did he think he was? The tirade was refreshing in its way. Rollison was humble and apologetic, and the soft answer did what it often does.

He was allowed to drive on.

Beck's car was parked near the garage. Rollison returned the Morris and walked towards the chalets of the Middle Camp. About him was a multitude, bent on having a good time.

Beck put up a good act, an "I can't be beaten" act, but he was taking a lot of chances while trying to frighten him, Rollison, off. It was a modified form of terror campaign, and could mean only one thing. Beneath that arrogant front, Beck felt unsafe. He was going to feel much more so.

Rollison began to smile.

He went to Elizabeth's chalet. He tapped, and she opened the door. She looked beautiful—as she always looked. She wore a green dress patterned with white flowers, not the regulation white dress and red coat.

She backed into the chalet, startled.

"Hallo," said Rollison, and beamed. "Forgive me yet?"

"I don't know what you mean."

She had obviously been expecting someone else, and was disappointed; was she also nervous; frightened? He wished he could make her talk. He half-wished that he hadn't tried to scare her into talking on the previous night. He remembered thinking that she might be just a *little* dumb.

"My ridiculous idea that you might have tied your stocking round Dick Middleton's neck," he said.

Her words came with a rush.

"Have you—found out who did?"

"Not yet. I hope you can help."

"I can't," she said. It was almost a whisper. "I can't tell you a thing. I know nothing." It was as if she had rehearsed a lesson, and this was the moment for its recitation.

He smiled—the kind of smile which could melt strong hearts. He drew nearer, took her arm, and spoke as a benevolent uncle might.

"Liz, I know you're worried and you've plenty on your

mind. Let me help. I don't have to tell the world, the Camp big shots, or the police, if it comes to that. First and last I'd like to help you. Let me. What do you know?"

It was all beautifully said; and futile.

"I know nothing," she insisted, and freed herself.

"Oh, come. Lovely creatures like you shouldn't go around scared of their own shadows or bad men or even boy friends who take the wrong turning."

It was no use.

"I'm not frightened, I—I'm scared in case something else should happen to Dick, after last night." That was her own mind, working; it hadn't worked very fast, which might be because she was living on her nerves. Certainly fear hadn't come suddenly; she had been nervous before, edgy—scared. Last night had simply brought everything to a head. "That's all." She added the last words defiantly.

"Lies, Liz," Rollison said. "Who will they help? Dick? Don't fool yourself. Tell me what it's all about."

His voice was cajoling, his smile should melt ice; but the girl stood very stiff, as if physically frightened.

"You're talking nonsense!"

"All right, Liz," he said sorrowfully. "If you won't help, don't blame anyone but yourself if things go wrong."

He was watching her very closely.

She bit her lips, but showed no sign of changing her mind. She even succeeded in meeting his eyes, and he reminded himself that he hadn't seen such beautiful eyes for —well, it must be two years.

He put a finger beneath her chin, pushed her face up, and kissed her, firmly. Then he backed away. Her eyes stormed at him, she raised her hand as if to slap his face; then let it drop.

"Get out of here," she breathed. "I hate the sight of you, get out!"

"Liz," Rollison said, "I'm human. You're beautiful. You're the most beautiful thing I've ever seen. I'd like to help you. I will help you, if I can—it'll be much easier if you'll tell me how I can. I'm the friend with no axe to grind. I'm the *only* man on this camp you can wholly trust. You can't be sure of any of the others, can you?"

She didn't speak.

"When you realize you've got to have help, come and tell me," Rollison said. "And Liz—I had to be sure you weren't bad, didn't I? I had to be sure that you hadn't put that stocking round Dick's neck, and twisted, twisted——"

"*Don't!*" she gasped.

"Now I'm sure you didn't," he said, blandly, "so I can promise you help. Don't forget—there isn't anyone else on the Camp whom you can trust. Not—one—single—person."

He turned and left her.

He wondered how much she knew, and what frightened her, and why she wouldn't talk of it. He thought of Cyrus Beck. He thought of a flat, menacing voice; a tall, lean figure in the shadows; black, frizzy hair; dark, burning eyes; and he felt the influence of the man.

How much more would a girl like Elizabeth feel it?

Or a man like Dick Middleton?

Were they both being blackmailed into helping, or at least into keeping silent, because they knew or had some idea about the fate of three missing Redcoats and one missing girl.

From a nearby shrubbery he waited for Liz to go out; that took ten minutes. No one was about when he slipped across to her chalet, and, using the master-key, went in.

He searched everywhere; moved the bed, the chest, table, everything; but he found nothing to help him, not a single dollar bill.

Outside the radio was sounding over the chalet top. Dancing—Holiday Princess—Tarzan—perfect visibility—hockey—would Mr. Ryall report to the office, please?—perfect visibility, why not see the Camp from the air? Don't forget the Holiday Princess Competition. Would Mr. Ryall . . .

Ryall.

Rollison turned smartly towards the offices, only five minutes' walk away. A broadcast for him meant an emergency.

He hurried past a children's playground, where the huge toy soldiers beamed down on them; soon, he was in the offices. Girls watched him, two or three clerks looked up and smiled. He could see Aird through the glass walls. The Camp Controller was standing up, so was Llewellyn; there was a big man with them—a man in a brown suit.

Rollison reached the door, and tapped.

"Come in," Aird said. He didn't smile. "Glad you've made it so quickly, Mr. Rollison—this is Inspector Davies of the local police."

Rollison switched on his party smile.

"Hallo, Inspector! Nice to see you."

"I'm glad to meet a man I've heard so much about," said Davies, with a lilting tone in his voice and a smile in his eyes which suggested that he meant what he said; and was also mildly amused, as a good policeman should always be amused by the Toff; or, for that matter, by any private eye.

The Welshman's smile faded into gravity.

"I'm hoping you'll be able to help me," he said, still with the lilt in his voice, "Mr. Aird thinks it's possible that you will be able to, now. It's about the girl, Susan Dell, who disappeared from here yesterday."

Rollison said softly, almost fearfully: "Yes?"

He felt sure what was coming.

"She's dead," said the Inspector.

Rollison felt a stab at his chest, as if from a sword. He saw a pair of lovely eyes, nearly as beautiful as Elizabeth's, gold with green flecks. They held appeal, too; Susan had wanted help, and he had failed her, and now she was dead.

This case *was* deadly.

How much had Aird told Davies?

"That's bad," he said. "That's the devil. How?"

"She appears to have fallen over the cliffs at Harlech," said the Inspector. He looked out of the window, as if to remind Rollison that Harlech was just across the water from the Camp. On a clear day one could see the famous castle whence the legendary Men had marched.

She *appeared* to have fallen . . .

"And Captain Aird tells me that you think you knew the man she was with, this man Clark," went on the Inspector. "Did you, Mr. Rollison?"

Aird hadn't said much, then; Aird was silently asking Rollison to be cautious.

"Yes," said Rollison promptly. "One of the odd things. He was a man named Horace Clark, who was sentenced to three years for a jewel-robbery. A London job—about six years ago, the trial was at the Old Bailey."

"Why, that will be a great help, it will indeed." Davies became enthusiastic; his manner suggested that there might be something in Toffs and private eyes after all. "I can get in touch with Scotland Yard and find the man, then."

"He's missing, is he?"

"Yes, indeed," said Davies, "he's missing—that is, we can't find out where he was last night."

"When did the girl die?"

"During the night it must have been, she fell from a height—on the rocks, near Harlech." Davies made it very clear. "Well, I'll worry you again if there's anything else you can help me with."

He shook hands; he thanked Rollison again; he assured Aird that he didn't want an escort to the car outside, but Llewellyn went with him.

Aird sat on the corner of his desk; a worried man.

"We could call him back and tell him more," he said as the door closed. "I didn't want to, until I'd had a word with you."

"Not yet." Rollison was almost brusque. "No case. The girl and the man with her both vanished—but if he doesn't connect that with the disappearing Redcoats, why should we make him?"

He didn't smile, but looked at the window. He could pretend that through the haze across the bay, he could see the angry rocks near Harlech; and the green-flecked eyes, closed now; a lovely body, flat and flabby; life, all hope of ecstasy, all beliefs and all fears gone.

How frightened she had been.

How frightened Elizabeth Cherrell was.

Aird said : "This has shaken me very badly, Rollison. I've been worried about it before, but this. Death—I suppose there's no point in assuming that it was murder. Davies didn't say much to suggest——"

"Let's assume it was murder," Rollison said. "Let's take it for granted that it's ugly and deadly—and that it might happen again. Give me twenty-four hours, and I'll have an answer, or else a strong case for asking the local police to bring the Yard in. One or the other, guaranteed."

"I'll speak to the Colonel," Aird said.

"Meanwhile, something to do," Rollison said. "We need someone who's absolutely trustworthy—two people in fact. One is to follow Elizabeth Cherrell, the other is to follow Middleton, wherever they go. We daren't risk more disappearances." He didn't add that from tonight he would be able to have these two watched by his own *aides* from the East End.

"I'll arrange that at once," Aird promised. "Two of my Security men will do—I'll take them off general work. Like to see them ?"

"Later, thanks," Rollison said. "They're not to let Elizabeth or Middleton know that they're being followed."

"No." Aird didn't ask why he named Elizabeth and the Redcoat leader.

Rollison told him what had happened during the night.

Llewellyn came in—broad, burly, looking rather more like a slightly smaller edition of Colonel Wickford White. He wore a kind of shocked frown.

"I say !" he breathed. "That's a bad business. Poor kid. I remember her, too, very nice looking. Rollison, you don't think it's anything to do with——" He broke off.

He wasn't a fool; he must know that Rollison thought that it might be something to do "with". Why had he said that? What was he trying to do—create too great an impression of his own sweet innocence ?

Rollison felt himself doubting the man's integrity.

He found himself doubting everyone as he went to see

Jolly. Even Jolly was behaving oddly because of a middle-aged woman clerk.

·   ·   ·   ·   ·

At ten minutes past one Rollison was at the door of Cyrus Beck's chalet. He had watched Beck and his wife leave for the dining-hall a few minutes before.

Rollison used his pick-lock blade, and stepped inside. He wasn't sure what he was looking for, only that he wanted a case against Beck which Beck couldn't duck.

He had no time to think, to be on guard. He had just time to feel fear——

Two men leapt at him from behind the door as he closed it. A third rushed from a corner.

CHAPTER XIV

THREE COULD DIE...

As they came, Rollison covered up, fighting down his surging alarm. Beck was really clever, Beck had expected him. He caught the first ringing blow, a cosh on the side of the head. It hurt; and it made him savage. He sent one man back with a pile-driver, but he was crowded out, he couldn't last long with the third man waiting to rush. Was Jolly——

Glass smashed, splintered, and flew.

"*Stop this!*" a man said firmly. "Stop, or I fire."

The clear, precise voice affected the nerves of the assailants as an atom bomb might strike a Pacific atoll. All activity ceased. All venom and all viciousness was drained out of the trio. They gaped at the window, where the glass had broken in the shape of a large star. Framed in this was Jolly triumphant. His right hand and arm were thrust forward; there was no doubting the business end of the automatic pistol which he held.

"I hope I'm not late, sir," he said apologetically. "As instructed, I waited in a nearby chalet, but the door stuck. Would you be good enough to open the door?"

Rollison had only to move his hand.

"Pleasure," he said.

"Now if you will take the gun," Jolly said, still framed, "I will gladly come and render any assistance you may require."

He beamed.

His voice had a song in it. He handed Rollison the gun, and disappeared. Three pairs of scared eyes transferred their gaze from Jolly, and the star of a frame, to Rollison. Two Campers came running, and Jolly was both earnest and convincing in his reassurances. They went off.

Rollison opened the door wider, cheerfully. It was comforting to know that he could still think a move or two ahead

of the Becks of the world; for Beck had obviously not expected Jolly to be waiting; and Beck himself would stay
away, anxious not to get mixed up in trouble at the Camp.

Poor Beck.

"We don't *know* these—ah—gentlemen, do we?" asked
Jolly; his tone was enough to make worms squirm.

"We've met on the road," Rollison said lightly. "They
tried this once before."

"How very foolish of them," Jolly murmured, and Rollison was sure that there was an amused gleam in his eyes.
"They should realize that they will *always* come unstuck
when they are opposing the Toff, shouldn't they? Have you
any instructions, sir?"

"We'll take them to your chalet, then make some long-
term plans," Rollison decided.

He looked at the gun. He looked at the men. As men,
there was nothing particularly unusual about them, although
one had a red scar on his right cheek and another a bald
patch in frizzy yellow hair. They were just hoodlums. They
had probably come from indifferent homes, won a scholar-
ship to Borstal, and graduated by degrees to a life which
was really a series of hops from one prison to another. There
was little to suggest that they would ever know the meaning of repentance, although they would doubtless cringe and
crawl in the hope of being let off lightly.

"You," Rollison said to the man with a bald patch, "follow my man out of the hut. Don't make any mistake, I'll
shoot if you run." He spoke quietly. He didn't scowl or
frown; he simply looked at them. The convincing factor was
in his eyes; a threat, a menace, a promise that he meant
exactly what he said.

They started from the chalet.

"Walk three abreast, and follow Jolly," Rollison ordered.

. . . . .

There were times when most things went easily. This was
one. Aird was in his office, alone. Yes, he could give them
the key of an empty chalet—one which was used for emer-

gencies. He sent the key to Rollison's chalet. Another procession followed, to the empty one, which was to serve as a prison. At Rollison's request, Aird's messenger brought plenty of rope. Jolly appeared to take an almost indecent pleasure in tying the prisoners up; and now and again a trifle from the air from *La Ronde* burst, as it were, from his lips. All this, Rollison noticed without comment.

He questioned the trio.

He knew their names, from papers he took from their pockets. There was nothing else to help him. They swore that they received their orders from Clark—not Beck. Beck wasn't mentioned. They successfully resisted trick questions, and there was no time to try strong-arm methods—yet. They could wait and, if necessary, could be used later, preferably after dark and probably when Bill Ebbutt—for long renowned for having the most disintegrating punch in the East End of London—was here to assist.

Rollison doubted if the trio knew much.

Their task, they said, was simply to beat him up and to put him out of action for a few days. Virtuously and vehemently they swore that no such thing as murder had been contemplated. For their services they had been paid twenty-five pounds each, plus their expenses. They were staying at Pwllheli; Clark had sent for them and told them to wait for his orders, which they swore they had received by telephone.

Beck had certainly given some, but probably they were frightened of Beck; too frightened to talk.

"We'll take their finger-prints," Rollison said, "and leave them. You brought the kit, didn't you?"

"Most assuredly, sir," said Jolly.

A quarter of an hour later, the prints had been taken and the trio were locked in the chalet, securely bound. Rollison went alone to Beck's chalet, which was still empty. He searched again.

The dollar bills were still there. So was a small gas pistol and a number of tiny plastic phials containing the gas.

Rollison began to hum to himself. He took the phials

outside and, using an awl-blade of his knife, pierced a tiny hole in each and then replaced them. Beck would be disappointed when next he used the gas pistol.

.   .   .   .   .

"Jolly," said Rollison.

"Sir," murmured Jolly.

"Neat work nicely done."

"A *pleasure,* sir. I'm glad you advised me to carry a gun, and earnestly recommend that you do the same from now on."

"I will. Susan Dell's dead."

The glow left Jolly's eyes, the smile left his lips.

They were in Rollison's chalet. It was nearly two o'clock. Outside, the sun was hot, the afternoon would be uncomfortably warm, the sea and the baths would probably be invaded by an all-time record crowd. Already people were running about, laughing and joking, the afternoon fun and games were on, and——

The radio started with the usual notices.

Music followed.

"I'm very sorry to hear about that, sir," Jolly said slowly. "It puts the finger down rather heavily, doesn't it. What do you propose to do next?"

"Tackle Beck. Openly."

Jolly didn't approve or disapprove.

"A false move from us, and three Redcoats might not live," Rollison said very slowly. "One thing to remember above the rest."

"Yes, sir," he said heavily. "There is, of course, one other thing which I expect you have considered."

"What's that?"

"They might already be dead. Beck might be——"

"Bluffing. Yes. How many times have you seen him?"

"Three."

"Impression?"

"I get——" Jolly hesitated, and then shrugged. "Perhaps I had best put it this way. I saw him once when I was with a lady from the Reception Desk, and without knowing who he was or that I was interested in him, my companion said : 'That man gives me the creeps.' "

"I see what you mean," Rollison said. "He's like an Old Testament prophet gone bad. No fool. And he's managed to get his wife to change dining-tables, so that she now sits opposite me. I distrust the obvious move. Don't you?"

"Yes, sir," Jolly said. "I get——" He paused.

"Yes."

"I think that I said something of the kind earlier," said Jolly. "I get an impression of something very clever, cunning, deep—may I use the word sinister?"

"Yes," said Rollison. "You may. Now get on the telephone to Grice at the Yard. If he's not there, speak to Patton, of finger-prints. Give them the main points of the finger-prints, and post the prints themselves to the Yard. We want to know if any of the three has a record, and for what kind of job."

"I understand, sir," murmured Jolly.

Rollison left the chalet a few minutes afterwards.

On the playing-fields young girls were playing hand-ball with a vigour which made him feel hot looking at them. There were crowds everywhere. Shrieking came from the swimming-pools. On another playing-field Uncle Pi and the Aunts and several *aides* were staging some kind of beauty competition; there must have been five hundred children within reach of Uncle Pi. He seemed unflustered and cool; no one else was. He even caught sight of Rollison, and nodded.

When Beck knew that his thugs had been tricked, what would he do?

Decide that things were too hot?

Rollison walked past some bushes. He wasn't being followed. Could Beck call on more men to help him?

A man stepped from the bushes, and fell into step beside him. Rollison didn't glance round, but was sharply aware of the man. Beck. They walked twenty yards before they came to the end of a chalet line, and the sun fell upon them. Rollison's shadow was tall; the shadow of the man beside him was inches taller.

They stopped.

Beck said : "Where are my men?"

Rollison said : "Resting. Didn't I warn you?"

"I warned *you*," Beck said, in the flat voice which sounded much the same as it had when it had been muffled the night before. "Three Redcoats could have their throats cut."

"A girl could be pushed over the cliffs, too," Rollison said very gently. "And your neck could be stretched. I'd like to select your hanging rope for you."

Beck sneered. He had small, yellow, wide-spaced teeth; his eyes burned. That was a trick, of course. He was all the things that a Lyceum melodrama of the 1900s would have wanted of its villain; his villainy should be laughable.

Rollison had a creepy feeling of disquiet.

"She fell," Beck said. "Listen, you're making a nuisance of yourself. I don't want to have more trouble with you. Those three Redcoats are alive. They happened to notice something I didn't want them to notice. When I've finished, they can come back and organize things for Billy Butlin's. But if you don't stop, I'll slit their throats. I'd never be hanged for it. No one would ever find their bodies."

He grinned.

The worst thing was the effect he had; a clammy kind of effect; stifling, oppressive. It was difficult to be flippant. It was easy to believe that he could carry out his threat; easier to see that he would. He felt on top, and could stay that way for a while. It might do him good to feel that Rollison was unnerved; give him an erroneous idea that he was winning.

So Rollison did not answer back.

"So clear out," Beck said, as if he felt that he could throw his weight about. "Or go and find yourself a bit of stuff and have fun with her. Don't worry me any more. And——"
He stopped. He looked down on Rollison. He went on very slowly : "Let my three men go, see. Or else——"

He drew his forefinger across his throat. It was a revolting gesture; it had all the trimmings of the old stage props, yet was horribly real. He even made a vicious noise in the back of his throat; and Rollison, who had heard the death rattle often enough, recognized that for a good simulation.

"See," Beck leered, and turned, and would have walked on.

He was falling for this bluff.

Rollison said : "All right, Beck, if that's the way you want it. There *are* jobs I can't handle."

Beck turned, and grinned.

"So I'll turn it in," Rollison said, and kept a poker face, "and pass it on. The police might be able to do it better."

Beck's grin faded. He moistened his lips. He was a forbidding scarecrow of a man, at least six feet four inches tall. In their deep sockets, his eyes seemed to reflect the burning glow of the sun.

"I don't *talk*," he said. "I act. I left orders. If I run into trouble——" He made the revolting gesture again; made the noise like a death rattle. "See?"

He turned and walked away.

He behaved as if he were quite sure that Rollison would not go to the police.

He probably wouldn't be feeling so happy if he knew that the gas phials were empty.

Rollison would have been much happier if he could have been sure that Elizabeth was safe.

He went towards his chalet.

CHAPTER XV

DECISION

IT was so hot that every movement was an effort. A few people walked about, limply; and many children ran. Rollison could feel envious towards them, but envy was unimportant. Cyrus Beck and his false hopes were vital.

He reached his chalet.

"If I were you, sir," said Jolly, from the communicating door, "I should have a swim, it is the only way to keep really cool. Don't you agree?"

"I don't think I feel like swimming," Rollison said, and looked up. "What——" He stopped.

He said, afterwards, that the one thing which really kept his mind alert during those few days was the remarkable transformation of his man. He had never known Jolly so skittish or so bouyant, and this was a revelation; and he had never before seen Jolly in a swim-suit. For some ridiculous, ludicrous reason, it was scarlet. It covered his impudent chest and torso, but his bony back was bare. His arms and legs, surprisingly plump, had the whiteness of legs which normally never see the light of day or feel the warmth of the sun.

Jolly, about to put on a bathing-wrap, looked mildly embarrassed.

"I have telephoned the Yard, sir," Jolly said. "One of the three sets of prints is identified—belonging to a Fred Morse, a cat-burglar who has done—ah—time. He specialized in jewels."

Rollison just stared at him, and said : "Where on earth did you get that outfit?"

"The suit I bought from the Camp Store," said Jolly primly, "and the wrap I borrowed from a—ah—friend, sir."

"Can you swim?"

"Oh, yes," said Jolly. "In my youth I was considered by my tutors to be most promising." He stopped.

He looked into Rollison's eyes, and sobered. His own eyes asked questions which Rollison recognized and answered.

"If he were the Devil himself, Beck couldn't be more sure that he's going to get away with it," he said.

"I think I know what you mean, sir."

"He even demands his three thugs back."

"Are you going to release them?" asked Jolly. He volunteered no opinion as to whether that would be good or bad tactics.

"No," Rollison said. "Not yet. We have to draw a line. We don't mind Beck deducing that we're nervous, but he doesn't have to think we're palsied with fear. Beck as Beck is a musical-comedy crook, but baiting him isn't the end of it." Rollison was almost gloomy as he lit a cigarette.

"One can obtain a certain zest from risking one's own life, but risking others is a very different matter," Jolly said, earnestly.

" 'Never send to know for whom the bell tolls'," Rollison quoted glumly. " 'It tolls for thee.' Yes. And Susan Dell's eyes will never glow with laughter again." He drew deeply at the cigarette. "What's wrong, Jolly? I can't get a grip. Clark's an ex-jewel thief, so is another of Beck's boys, there are a lot of dollars about, but the rest is guesswork. As for people—Middleton is elusive and vague; Elizabeth Cherrell is like a wraith. They aren't like real people, they're——"

"Dictated to by fears," Jolly said soberly. "Terrified."

"Fear of Beck."

"He could affect some people like that." Jolly was cautious.

"I've checked on Middleton and Elizabeth today," Rollison went on, abruptly. "They've met twice. Nothing's happened. Elizabeth had the morning off, but is helping to supervise the Beauty Contest this afternoon. None of the other Redcoats appear to be affected—except possibly Uncle Pi, who is in love with Elizabeth."

"You haven't yet had a heart-to-heart talk with Uncle Pi, have you?" Jolly murmured.

"Think it's worthwhile?"

"I think I do, sir," Jolly hazarded. "I have a little information of some interest. It was Camp Staff gossip that Miss Cherrell and the missing Redcoat Campion were very friendly."

"Oh, *were* they."

"Yes, sir. I am now doing all I can to find out more about other men who appear to have been attracted by Miss Cherrell. So far we know that Campion, Wray—or Uncle Pi— and Middleton have all been attracted."

"In love with her do you mean?" Rollison eyed his man intently. "Are you trying to make out that Liz Cherrell is a kind of *femme fatale*?"

"Hardly that, sir. But Campion was certainly attracted to her before he disappeared, Middleton is clearly fearful of some disaster while being in love with her, and we may find that Miss Cherrell is in fact the common factor."

Jolly smoothed down his sparse grey hair, and darted a glance at the clock on his dressing-chest. That was unheard of; it was epochal, even revolutionary—Jolly never eyed the clock when he was with Rollison, for he had no time of his own.

"In a hurry, Jolly?" asked Rollison, with hardly perceptible sarcasm.

"Not exactly in a hurry," Jolly said blandly, "but I am keeping a lady waiting, and she has been extremely helpful. Arrangements are now made for Ebbutt and his men to have accommodation. But she will understand, I'm sure." Jolly was earnest as he moved forward. "May I suggest, sir, that the chief reason you find it difficult to get a grip is the nature of the conditions here? Everyone is having a wonderful time, everyone is concentrating on *enjoyment,* the gaiety is non-stop, and yet there is this stalking fear, this eeriness, the awareness of impending disaster. It doesn't seem real, and because of the touch of fantasy, it worries you more than you need be worried."

Jolly stopped.

Rollison drew a deep breath.

"Wonderful," he said. "You are promoted to my personal psychiatrist. Don't keep your lady friend waiting any longer."

"I won't, sir," said Jolly with alacrity. "I seriously recommend that a swim, even a few minutes cooling off in the water, would do you a great deal of good."

He went off.

Rollison stubbed out his cigarette. Jolly had some reason for seeing his lady on time; Jolly had also suggested that Liz Cherrell might be less dumb than deadly.

Rollison used the telephone. Llewellyn told him that Uncle Pi was with several boat-loads of children going across to Harlech. This was a regular trip for members of the Beaver Club. Rollison's lips tightened as a picture of a woman's body crushed and broken by the rocks sprang to his mind.

Middleton and Elizabeth Cherrell were somewhere about the Camp, Rollison was told.

"Nothing new," Rollison said sadly to himself. Then the telephone bell rang with a call from London, and hopes soared.

It was Grice.

"Here we go, spending public money like water," Rollison chided. He sounded like Davies, with a lilting voice. "Heard from Inspector Davies, now, man?"

"That's right," Grice said. "I've been checking, Rolly. Clark and the man Morse had been in jewel rackets, and it's known that a lot of stolen jewels are being sold in the U.S.A. against dollars which are smuggled into the country and sold on the black market at a high premium. That could be the game."

Rollison said quietly: "Yes. Thanks, Bill."

"Pleasure. Now, this girl-friend of Clark's—Susan. We can't find out anything about her, and Clark's still missing. It looks an ugly job. Made any more progress?"

"Only taken three prisoners and saved a life or so," said Rollison, airily.

"Seriously—anything new?"

"No. Anything known about Beck?"

"Nothing," said Grice. "But I've made a check on Red-coat leader, Middleton."

"Ahh!" breathed Rollison.

"He hasn't a wife."

All the foolery faded from Rollison's mind.

"*What?*"

"It's a fact," Grice said. "I can't find a thing about him apart from that, and if it were a crime not to be married, there'd be another reason for putting you inside."

"Then you'd never get results," said Rollison unkindly. "Thanks, Bill. 'Bye."

He rang off, and was very thoughtful indeed. If Middleton weren't married, why did he say that he was? One question was answered : it wasn't surprising that Middleton had laughed so wildly when Rollison had asked if his wife were in the Camp.

Why claim that a non-existent wife had left him?

The answer might be found, soon. Grice's theory could be right, and was certainly worth thinking about, although it was almost too hot to think.

Beck would soon make another move—and Rollison meant to wait for it. Middleton and Elizabeth were both being watched, what could happen to them?

He decided to have a swim; when he was cooler his thoughts might have more point.

.   .   .   .   .   .

There was a moment, at the side of the swimming-bath positively teeming with people, when Rollison doubted the wisdom of coming. He climbed to the top diving-board. Beneath him there was just room to cleave the water. He went down cleanly; and the dive and the immersion exhilarated him. He dived from the high board half a dozen times and, by then, was being watched from all sides.

He caught sight of Jolly, disporting himself with the grey-haired woman with the attractively wrinkled face; Jolly did not appear to see him. He stopped diving, and swam the length of the bath. Now his head bumped a body, now his foot kicked a head, now his hand struck an arm; there was hardly room, but he managed. Standing at the shallow end, brushing the hair from his forehead, he caught a glimpse of Rosa Beck.

She was sitting in a chair by the side of the swimming-pool, looking at him. She wore a brief swim-suit, as scarlet as Jolly's. At a distance, she looked younger than she was.

She smiled. Rollison waved, then dived in again. As he went, he thought he saw the big and burly man who had tried to beat him up at the Viennese Bar. Rickett.

Rollison started to swim.

He felt something clutch his ankle.

That did not alarm him. At first he just waited to be freed. Then he tried to shake himself free. Next he felt himself being pulled down into the water.

That was when he felt panic.

He kicked out, but couldn't free himself—and a weight descended on his back. He went under. He was vaguely aware of the swimming, diving, laughing, shrieking mass of people and children; of the great weight on his back. He opened his eyes, and as through a distorting mirror he could see arms and legs and bodies, all moving drunkenly—but he couldn't see what was holding him. He held his breath, but would soon have to breathe; or swallow water.

The weight pressed on his head. He was being held under; *pushed down.*

His head began to swim, and he felt great pain as the pressure at his lungs increased. He kicked out again, and fancied that the pressure at his ankle eased a trifle. He kicked and struck. The movements of his arms in the water were slow, puny, futile; but he touched something. He made himself keep still, and opened his eyes. He saw an arm close to him, and a man's body, distorted by the water. Slowly, he found and twisted the wrist—while his lungs felt like bursting. The weight went from his head and back, and he bobbed up to the surface. He gasped for breath, took in a mouthful of water, and felt panic as he went down again.

He soon came up.

He fought against panic, won, struck out, and reached the side. He clung to the bar, gasping for breath; retching. He could hardly see. There was chatter and laughter in his ears, and the splashing of water; it seemed as if his head and his ears were filled with water and noise.

Gradually, his head cleared, and he could distinguish people. He saw the big and burly Rickett not far away, waist deep in water and leering at him. He saw Rosa Beck, smiling at him—almost anxiously. He saw no one else. He couldn't be sure whether that had been an attempt to drown or to frighten him.

Then he saw Beck.

The man walked past without glancing towards him, with his big pipe in his lips; a sinister scarecrow, looking out of place among the crowds in their swim-suits; as if he could not know the meaning of enjoyment.

Beck disappeared.

His wife was still smiling at Rollison—tensely.

Rollison climbed out of the bath, found his towel on the grass near by, and rubbed himself down gently. He was much cooler. He didn't feel sick; but he felt worse than he had when he had started out—all the exhilaration had gone. He would have to be very careful indeed with Beck.

Rosa came towards him. She wore a white wrap over the scarlet swim-suit, open at the front. No one could doubt the magnificence of her figure. Instead of looking less attractive in this undress, she looked more attractive. She hadn't bathed or thought of bathing, her make-up was very good.

She reached him.

"Hallo," she said, "enjoy your swim?" Her voice was husky.

"No," Rollison said.

There was something different about her; a kind of tension which he hadn't noticed before. It reminded him of Susan Dell. She hadn't Susan's eyes, but——

"I saw what happened." She spoke in a whisper, and

glanced over her shoulder, as if she were fearful of being heard. "I nearly——" She broke off.

"Nearly came to my rescue." He couldn't keep the sneer out of his voice.

She drew a deep breath.

"They—they were watching me, or I would have! They're always watching me. I daren't do a thing, I'm frightened all the time. But—if you know how I *hate* Beck!"

Rollison could only just hear those last words—yet they burned on her lips. "If you know how I *hate* Beck." Rollison looked into her eyes, seeking the truth. They seemed to glow with a reflection of the fire in Beck's. Was this true, or was it another move in Beck's plan to drive him away? He could let her think he was jittery, for she would probably tell Beck, and Beck might get over-confident.

"And how they scare me," she added abruptly.

"Then why come to my table? Why——"

"He sent me," she said. "I was to lead you up the garden." There was no smile, no hint that she realized the irony of the statement. She seemed in deadly earnest—as Susan had. "I must talk to you, but I'm watched all the time. He can lip read. Can you suggest where——" She broke off, helplessly.

Rollison said: "I'll think about it, and try to fix something by dinner."

"You must." She put her hand on his arm again, glancing about her, as if she were in fact fearful of being watched. "Susan wanted——" She broke off.

The big, brutish Rickett came towards them, wearing a black swim-suit and carrying a towel. He flicked the towel; the end caught Rollison's arm, and stung. The man sneered as he passed.

Rosa Beck went white.

"You see," she said. "It's hopeless."

"How were you to fool me, if we aren't allowed to talk to each other?" Rollison asked.

It was the obvious question. But the odd thing, which did more than anything else to suggest that she was genuine, was the fact that she behaved like this, that her nerves seemed to be so ragged.

"He changed his mind," she said. "I was to make you fall for me in a big way, and then he changed his mind. I think——" She licked her lips. "I *think* he guesses what I'll do if—if I can. He's uncanny, he can almost read my thoughts. And he thinks he has you on the run. But—I must see you, we must——" She stopped.

Not far away, Beck was approaching, and looking at them. It was almost possible to believe that his eyes were boring into his wife's mind; reading her thoughts.

She withdrew her arm from Rollison's.

Beck drew nearer.

"Do you know where the missing Redcoats are?" Rollison asked sharply. "Kick my ankle if you do."

She didn't move, but said hoarsely: "Don't let anything happen to me. Don't let it happen to me."

Beck walked past; until the last moment, his eyes were burning at his wife, but he didn't nod or speak or do anything to suggest that he knew her.

When he was out of earshot, Rosa said in a shaky voice:

"Don't let anything happen to me, Mr. Rollison. After this, anything might . . ."

CHAPTER XVI

THIN AIR . . .

"Nothing can happen to you out here," Rollison said, and then remembered what had happened in the swimming-pool. "Stay with the crowd. Wait here for half an hour, and I'll have someone follow you. You'll be all right."

"Did you—see how he looked at me?" She was shivering. It was possible, if difficult, to feign a shiver.

"Forget it."

"You don't know him," she breathed.

She broke off.

"Stay with the crowd," Rollison urged.

He left her, and didn't look back, although he sensed that she was watching him. He believed that if he looked into her eyes, he would see a measure of fear—but it might be faked fear. She was good; Cyrus Beck was good; deadly. She had played on the same string, the one string which struck a cord to which Rollison was really sensitive.

A Redcoat stopped him.

"Have you seen Liz Cherrell lately?"

"No. Why?" Rollison was sharp.

"She was looking for you." The Redcoat grinned. "Seemed to think it was a matter of life and death. How do you manage it?"

Rollison made himself grin.

"Where was she?"

"Near your chalet—I think she left a note."

Rollison almost ran to his chalet.

Yes, Liz had left a note, brief, almost despairing. But it wasn't alarming, it gave him reason to hope that she was going to talk.

"I must see you, you were right," she'd written. "I'll be in my chalet."

So now she believed that he was the only man she could trust.

He hurried to her chalet, but she wasn't there. He started towards the offices at the double, when another Redcoat shouted :

"Oi, Ryall !" They were near the Mirror Bar. "You're wanted—Aird's office."

"On my way," Rollison called.

The radio was broadcasting, but he had become so used to it that he only heard what he wanted to hear. A flight was about to start, the free transport was waiting. The big reception hall was almost deserted; the offices weren't. He hurried to Aird's. Llewellyn was there by himself, pale, no longer boisterous. He looked pale; he looked frightened.

"Now what ?" Rollison asked, sharply.

"Rollison——"

He didn't finish. Foosteps sounded, as of a man running. Rollison looked up. It was Middleton, coming along the passage. Something in Middleton's manner started the old fears in Rollison; here was something that had gone badly wrong; more reason for fear.

Middleton burst in.

"Where is she ?" he demanded in a voice that quivered. "What have you done with her ? This is another of your foul games." He paused, then shouted : "*Where is she?*"

Rollison felt himself going cold.

Elizabeth——

"Dick, keep your head, for heaven's sake," said Llewellyn. There was a little more strength in his voice, but no less pallor in his cheeks. "Rollison, Elizabeth Cherrell——"

"She's vanished !" Middleton cried.

"Just disappeared into thin air," Llewellyn said.

Middleton gripped Rollison's arm; his fingers covered exactly the same spot that Rosa Beck's had done. The fear in his eyes might be the same as Rosa's—fear of Beck.

"This is your crazy idea ! Where——"

"No," Rollison said. "It shouldn't have happened. She was being followed——"

"Knocked out," Llewellyn said.

"You know where she is!" breathed Middleton. "Tell me, or I'll smash your face in."

"The man who was watching her, I mean," Llewellyn said chokily. "He's in the First Aid rooms, now. Very nasty head. *Dick, don't be a fool!*"

"But Rollison knows."

"Nonsense! Dick, keep your head. We can't have everybody worried. If you go on like this the whole Camp——"

"What the hell do you think I care about the Camp? I want Elizabeth. Rollison——" Middleton dropped Rollison's arm. He seemed quite beside himself, shouting, making the men and girls in the offices stare through the windows. His face was pale and his eyes too bright; feverish. "I told you what I'd do!"

He smashed a blow at Rollison's face.

Rollison moved his head; the fist whistled past. He caught Middleton's wrist, twisted, and helped Middleton on his way. Middleton was thrown forward, partly by the twist, partly by the impetus of his own movement. He crashed against the wall, and the glass partitions shook.

Two Redcoats in the passages began to run.

Middleton crouched on the floor.

"We can't go on like this," Llewellyn said helplessly. "He's not himself, Rollison, he's half-crazy with anxiety. You don't——" He moistened his lips. "You *don't* know where Elizabeth is, do you?"

"No."

The two Redcoats were at the door, which was ajar. They came in. Rollison had seen them before—youngish fellows, one dark and the other fair. They looked spruce, too; and also anxious.

"Mr. Llewellyn——" One spoke to Aird's assistant as he looked at the Redcoat Captain on the floor. "Is it true that Liz Cherrell's disappeared?"

"I——"

"Ask him where she is," Middleton said hoarsely. He pointed a quivering finger at Rollison. "If he hadn't interfered it would never have happened to her. Ask him."

"Is this true, sir?" One of the Redcoats asked.

He was very young. He sounded as if he were talking to a don at his seat of learning—respectful but firm. He was a tough-looking young man, with something in his eyes which wasn't so much fear as apprehension; the beginning of fear.

"Poppycock," Rollison said. "But Liz is missing. A Security man was watching, apparently he——"

"Battered about the head," Llewellyn said. "Terrible."

"Where?"

"In one of the lounges. A Camper went in and heard him groaning. Awful. Before long——"

Llewellyn's disconnected sentences, his unsteady lips, his darting eyes, suggested that he was really losing his nerve. Where was Aird?

"As a matter of fact," the dark-haired youth said, "it's spreading round the Camp. The woman who found him went rushing out crying murder. Scared a lot of people. If you ask me, it isn't going to do any good. People *do* get scared. And there are a lot of rumours running around, you know, about disappearing Redcoats."

"*Must* be stopped," Llewellyn muttered.

"Where's Aird?"

"Gone to Shrewsbury," Llewellyn said. "He's meeting the Colonel there, possibly Mr. Butlin as well. We *can't* have panic. I don't know what to do."

"*I* know." That was Middleton, from the floor. The fair-haired Redcoat went across and started to help him up. "Get rid of Rollison."

"Oh, come." That was the dark-haired lad. "Can't do that—we need the Toff! Between you and me, sir," he said to Rollison, "there is going to be a lot of anxiety in the Camp as this spreads. It's been going around for some time, but hasn't really affected anyone. Now news of the attempt on Middleton's life has leaked out, and someone recognized you and said you wouldn't be here unless there were serious trouble. It's a kind of thing in the air, so to speak. Edginess. I sensed it at lunch-time. People looking over their shoulders, if you know what I mean. And now this attack on a Security man, and Liz vanishing—we just can't keep it quiet."

"Must," barked Llewellyn.

The two youngsters were helping Middleton up.

"I'd like to see where the man was attacked and then have a word with him," Rollison said. He smiled at Middleton. "Dick, I want to find Liz just as badly as you do. Take it easier."

Middleton muttered something and turned away, limping. The two young Redcoats looked at Rollison as if to say, "We understand, sir," and went out with him. Rollison felt a curious flatness at the "sir" and the attitude of deference. But that soon passed.

"I'll come with you," Llewellyn said.

"Another job to do first," Rollison said. "We want Mrs. Beck followed. Have to use a Security man. Send one over to me, will you, I'll be at the far end of the pool."

He hurried back to the spot where he had left Rosa.

    .   .   .   .   .

All Rollison could do was have a search started for Rosa—and go with Llewellyn to see the Security man who had followed Elizabeth and been found in a corner of one of the Quiet Lounges—there were several in the Camp. This one, near the main gates, had three doors leading into it. The man had been found behind two armchairs. There were bloodstains on the wall and on the back of a chair; but nothing that Rollison could see to help him find the identity of the attackers.

The man himself couldn't help.

Elizabeth Cherrell had gone into a quiet lounge to get some cards ready for an evening Whist Drive. The Security man had waited for ten minutes; she hadn't come out, so he had gone in. He hadn't seen Liz, but had been struck on the head while passing through the doorway.

Now he was heavily bandaged, and there was a bruise on the right cheek.

And Elizabeth was gone . . .

He gave Rollison a list of her movements; he had it all down, with a time-table. At first sight it did nothing to help —but there it was, the people she had seen and spoken to, the places she'd been to, a complete record of where she had been and what she had done from the moment that the man had started to watch her.

She had twice seen Middleton.

Rollison checked with the Security Officer who had followed Middleton; the two meetings between the Redcoat Captain and Elizabeth tallied on each record—they had met once in a dining-hall, once on the playing-fields.

Rollison talked to the gate officials, within sight of the Quiet Lounge. Neither of the men on duty had noticed anything unusual. It must have happened very quickly. The windows were visible from the gate, but of course the men had to look out of the Camp, not inwards.

Had there been anything at all unusual?

Nothing.

Who had gone in and out of the Camp?

A lot of cars, of course—but no record was kept, the gate-keepers simply made sure that no one without authority came *in*. But they were observant. There had been an R.A.C. scout at the gate about the time of the disappearance, and he was telephoned, to help. Rollison left them making up a list, from memory, of all the vehicles which had gone out of the gates. Of course, Elizabeth could have been in any car—no matter how small. If she had been on the floor, with a rug thrown over her, there would have been little chance of her being seen. She *could* have walked out, of course, without using the main entrance; but that wasn't likely.

Was it? What would Jolly say?

More reports came in.

Cyrus Beck hadn't been out of the Camp. Nor had the brutish Rickett. Rosa wasn't in her chalet.

The three prisoners were still in theirs.

Rollison left the gates, for the offices. He soon sensed something which he hadn't noticed earlier: he was being

E

watched by a lot of people. It wasn't the same kind of thing that had made him sensitive to Beck, not cause for fear; yet there was something furtive about it.

He was being pointed out by many people.

He heard a boy in his early teens say: *"That's him, Mum."*

People stopped and looked round when he passed; or stopped to watch him as he approached. Children pointed. It revealed something which had not existed in the Camp the previous day, and told Rollison that the dark-haired Redcoat had known what he was talking about.

He went to his chalet, but Jolly wasn't there.

He telephoned the gate and was told that at least twenty-seven cars had left the Camp, as well as several Camp lorries and vans; it was impossible to be sure that everyone was on the list.

Jolly arrived, still in his wrap.

He listened as he dressed.

"I haven't been idle, sir," he said, as if he were conscious of censure. "I've been trying to find out whether there *is* any common factor in the disappearances. Apart, I mean, from people involved in each. I think there is one, and the place where Miss Cherrell was last seen is consistent."

"What is it?"

"All of the missing Redcoats were last seen near the main gates," Jolly said. "My—ah—friend has been very helpful, making inquiries as discreetly as she could, but that hasn't been wholly successful. Here is the list, sir."

He had it written down.

Jim Campion had been seen by the assistant at a sweet-shop, near the main gates—or had been last noticed. Tommy Tucker had been seen at the entrance to the Princes Theatre, almost opposite the shop. Peverill had been on the nearby putting-course.

There was another note in Jolly's clear handwriting.

Elizabeth Cherrell had been seen with each of the three Redcoats a little while before they had vanished; she herself had made this clear.

"What else do we know?" Rollison asked heavily.

"One other common factor has come to light, sir," Jolly said. "I think I may say that my helper has done a *remarkable* job." He was firm. "It is now certain that each man—Campion, Tucker, and Peverill—was very friendly with Miss Cherrell; they were rivals, one might say. She did not discourage or strongly encourage them, as far as I can find out."

"How did you find this out?"

"It was common knowledge to the Redcoats, sir. However, these men were all at one time or other assistants to Uncle Pi, when looking after the elder children."

"Oh," said Rollison heavily.

"There is still another factor," Jolly went on serenely. "Everyone, including Miss Cherrell, must have been in the plain view of dozens, if not hundreds of people, just before they vanished. It is almost as if they just walked out. But not one of them was seen to pass through the gates by the gate-keepers. The disappearances were about that spot, all the same—a spot from which they could go or be taken out of the Camp very easily."

"Or taken to any other part of the Camp," Rollison pointed out. "The railway—the beach—the fields on either side. The trouble here is that no one ever watches anyone—so many people are moving about, you just don't notice them unless there's some special reason for it. We need Ebbutt and his boys."

Ebbutt and his men couldn't easily be knocked out, but—were they coming too late?

"Are you going to tackle Middleton again, sir?" asked Jolly.

"He's hardly responsible for what he says, but yes. But first I want to see Uncle Pi. Any more low-down on him?"

"He's extremely popular with everyone, sir—and all know that he is deeply in love with Miss Cherrell. Apparently he has been for years. There is a section of Camp opinion which believes his slight deformity puts him out of the running, as it were."

"H'm, yes. A man with a grievance like that could be a psychological case," Rollison said gloomily. "Keep an eye on him yourself when you can spare the time, Jolly." The sarcasm appeared to go over Jolly's head. "I want to have another go at Beck, but I'll wait until our reinforcements arrive tonight. But no longer, Beck's due for his shock. And——"

The telephone bell rang.

He grabbed the receiver.

"Rollison here . . ."

He wasn't surprised when he heard Llewellyn's voice; he wasn't surprised really when he heard the Assistant Controller say:

"That Mrs. Beck—she's been found, Rollison. Down in the rock garden by the railway. Strangled."

CHAPTER XVII

CAUSE FOR FEAR

ROSA BECK wasn't dead.

The hideous similarity between the attack on her and the attack on Middleton couldn't be missed. A cord, not a stocking, had been tied round her neck, and it looked as if she had been left for dead. Two Sisters from the Sick Bay had rushed to her, and a doctor was on his way from Pwll-heli when Rollison reached the rock gardens.

There were dozens of people about, mostly middle-aged or elderly, seeking coolness in the shade and beauty among the flowers. It was always quiet here, except for a few very young children in prams or in their mothers' arms. When Rollison arrived, there were at least a hundred people.

He felt their gaze.

"There he is. . . ."

"That's Rollison."

"That's the *Toff*."

"Murder . . ."

He sensed the feeling which Llewellyn had earlier; one which probably explained Llewellyn's anxiety and the fact that he had almost lost his grip. Here was the beginning of fear among the Campers. Here was a fat chrysalis of rumour which would soon grow wings.

" *Murder . . . Strangled . . . Detectives . . . The Toff . . . Murder . . . Murder—One last Night . . . Disappeared they have . . .*"

He did not hear the actual words, but sensed them, as if thoughts in the minds of the people could be projected into his.

He searched for clues. There were a few footprints, with nothing remarkable about them. The paths and steps on the large rock-gardens were of stone; most of the flower-beds were so crammed with flowers that feet could only trample these down, not leave tell-tale signs behind.

Rosa, now in the hospital, had been found behind some bushes.

She must have walked down a path from the road at the end of the chalets, and been attacked from behind. The actual spot had been cleverly chosen, the most remote in the garden.

Llewellyn arrived.

"Must have the police in, of course," he said. "Aird telephoned me, just before you came. He thinks so, too. I'll telephone Davies. Yes?"

"Yes," Rollison agreed.

"What made you think she might be attacked?"

Rollison said : "She'd asked for help but didn't wait for it. Like Susan Dell." He looked bleakly across the garden and to the railway tracks.

"She'll pull round," Llewellyn said. "Think she can help?"

"If she were in a mind to, but this might scare her off," Rollison said. "Can we blame anyone for not wanting to be murdered?"

"Shocking," Llewellyn said weakly. "And here, of all places—it's inconceivable ! Haven't you *any* idea what it's about?"

"No."

"I'll telephone Davies," Llewellyn said. "He'll soon be here. Certainly can't wait any longer before we call the police, but"—he seemed to be talking in order to convince himself—"what effect it's going to have on the Campers I don't know. If they get an idea that a murderer's loose . . ." He looked really dismayed. "If you knew how rumour spreads in a place like this . . ."

He didn't finish, but hurried off.

The dark-haired and the fair-haired young Redcoats who had been with them earlier were with the crowd now. So were several others. Uncle Pi, with a dozen or so children about him, was on the playing-fields near the chalets.

By then, Rollison had absorbed the reason for Llewellyn's fear, and accepted it as logical. If rumour that a killer was at large spread far and wide, it would soon be distorted. The killer would turn into a man who would strike at anyone; anywhere. It would become a Thing. The danger of panic working itself into people's hearts, minds, eyes, voices, was haunting Llewellyn.

Rollison went to Middleton's chalet, but Middleton wasn't there. He turned and saw Uncle Pi approaching.

"Rollison, I was just coming to see you."

"Nice of you," Rollison said. "I wanted——"

"Dick Middleton, as you're at his chalet. He's in mine." Rollison went to Uncle Pi's chalet. "We were both coming to see you." The hunchback looked very white, especially about the lips. Was it pain in his eyes? "Any idea where Liz is, yet?"

"No."

"Dick has an idea about you," Uncle Pi said. "He thinks that you're lousy."

Middleton was standing by the side of Uncle Pi's bed, smoking; his hands weren't steady, his eyes were glassy. Without the scarf round his neck, the red swelling showed how tight the stocking had been.

"That's right," he said. "Rollison, how *did* you get into my chalet last night?"

"I picked the lock."

Middleton said in a taut voice: "I'll tell you something else you did. You put a blanket over my head, then knocked me out, and then pretended to strangle me with Liz's stocking. *Then* you did your life-saving act. That's what I think of you."

"Crazy, you see," said Uncle Pi. His brown eyes were very bright. "Isn't he?"

He seemed to be asking the question of himself; and trying to seek an answer at the same time. The question was: *Can Dick Middleton be right?*

"Quite crazy," Rollison said.

"All right," growled Middleton, "explain how you happened to come along just at that moment? Go on. You wanted to appear a hero, and then——"

"Yes, and what then?" Rollison asked lightly. "I'd be interested to hear what motive I had."

"You know——" Middleton stopped.

"Let's assume I don't know a thing."

"*Assume?*" Uncle Pi could be bitingly sardonic.

"You knew damned well I've been trying to find out where the other fellows went," Middleton shouted. "You knew that I——"

He couldn't finish.

"So you're a detective too," Rollison said. That was meant to sting Middleton into saying more. "What else did I know?"

"You knew I was afraid that Liz was involved," Middleton said. He sounded as if the words choked him; and Uncle Pi looked as if he would willingly strangle him. "And you wanted to worm the truth out of me, wanted to find out how much I did know."

"Well, how much do you?"

"I just . . ." Middleton's voice seemed to die to a husky burr. He didn't actually form words for several moments. Uncle Pi continued to look at him. "I just suspected Liz," Middleton managed at last. "I hated myself for it, but——"

"Go on."

"She was friendly with the three who disappeared," Middleton burst out. "I know she was—she was stringing them along. She made them think there was a chance for them. The same as she did me. I——"

"Dick," said Uncle Pi, in the softest voice, "I ought to wring your neck for that, except that too many necks appear to have been wrung." His eyes were glowing. "And also except that I can see you're crazy. Give me one reason for suspecting Liz of any part in this devilry, apart from the fact that she was friendly with the three Redcoats who vanished."

"Isn't that enough?" Middleton rasped.

"No."

"I talked to her about them," Middleton said, as if goaded into going on. "She just brushed me off. Everyone else here was worried about it, when they had time to be worried, but Liz wasn't. She tried to make out that it was nothing to worry about, although——"

"Although what?"

Middleton went on hoarsely: "I can't help it if you're fooled by her, too! She's so beautiful that it *blinds* you. She can hypnotize you. When she wants anything——"

Uncle Pi thrust his hands deeper in his pockets.

"I can't stand this any more," he growled. "Or else I shall really wring his neck."

He went out.

Middleton glared after him.

Rollison said very mildly: "Do you love her as much as that, Dick?"

The Redcoat Captain didn't speak.

"She is lovely," Rollison said. "She might be a Delilah, too. But I didn't strangle you, you know. Not my cup of tea at all. Who put that idea into your head?"

Middleton didn't speak.

"Who?" Rollison insisted.

"She—she did," Middleton uttered. "And I almost believed her. It wasn't until I started talking to Uncle Pi that I realized that a man with your reputation——" He broke off, snatched a packet of cigarettes from his pocket, found it empty, growled: "Oh, hell!" and flung it at the wall. "I feel as if I *am* going crazy. If she's guilty, it's awful. If she's really missing——"

"Listen," Rollison said, putting a cigarette between Middleton's fingers. "What makes you think it possible that she was right, and that I attacked you?"

"Call me crazy," Middleton said. "I can't help it, perhaps I *am* crazy. But as soon as you arrived, you started going around with her. She was detailed to help you, but it seemed obvious that you knew each other."

Rollison didn't speak.

"I think it was obvious, anyhow," Middleton growled.

"She was with you all the time, you were always in a huddle. I could have broken your damned neck!" He drew fiercely at the cigarette, hesitated, then went on in a low-pitched, savage voice: "It's like living in hell. Loving her so much and believing that she's bad. Understand, fearing that she's *bad*. Is she? Tell me that, Rollison, *is* she?"

"We're finding out," Rollison said.

A few minutes later he went out of the chalet with Middleton. Uncle Pi was on one of the paths. Middleton went into his own chalet. Rollison went on, and Uncle Pi fell into step with him. They walked along in silence, until:

"Certain amount of confusion in Dick's mind, isn't there?" Uncle Pi said calmly. "Anyone who could believe ill of the Toff must be crazy!"

He gave the sardonic smile. With his slightly humped back and slightly twisted neck, he could look almost sinister —if it weren't for his wonderful voice and his honest eyes.

"Confusion, yes," Rollison said. "He might not be so crazy about Liz."

"I don't regard you as a sick man," Uncle Pi said with his wry smile. "I wouldn't mind punching you on the nose, and I want to punch someone."

"Go ahead."

They went towards the offices. Rollison was watched, pointed at, whispered about. There was a factor which he hadn't known before: people were subdued. The laughter of some people seemed forced. Rollison knew that much of this might be auto-suggestion; but not all of it. Those who were easily unnerved were already beginning to feel the strain. This showed among the Redcoats, too. Those who approached looked at Rollison almost longingly, as if asking:

"*Can't* you stop it?"

Not far behind them was Jolly; obviously watching Uncle Pi.

"Pi," Rollison said, as they reached the office, "I want you to get all the Redcoats together unofficially. Tell them that we're going to have a bit of panic on our hands if we're not careful, and drill them into handling it. Ask 'em what they think is the best thing to do, tell 'em that the reputation of the Camp is in their hands. You know the stuff."

"I see what you mean," Uncle Pi said slowly.

"And then I shall tell Aird that we need you to start work on pacifying the Campers," Rollison went on. "You can make more magic with that voice of yours. Just calm them down."

"I'll try," Uncle Pi said.

"Thanks. I don't know how you get all Redcoats together, but try to fix it before dinner, will you," Rollison asked.

"Right," said Uncle Pi.

Rollison turned into the offices. Uncle Pi went on; and behind him was Jolly and a crocodile of a dozen children. Rollison watched them and Uncle Pi, with his rounded shoulders and swift yet unhurried walk. Llewellyn, Colonel Wickford White, and another man whose face was in shadow were in Aird's office when Rollison went in.

"Where's Davies?" he asked dryly. "Don't we need him to make up the party?"

"He's with Mrs. Beck," Aird said. "Trying to find out what she knows. And his men are questioning Beck."

CHAPTER XVIII

POSSIBILITY

So the police were with the Becks.

And Beck could have three Redcoats killed; and perhaps Liz Cherrell, also.

Rollison found himself lighting a cigarette automatically. He had known that this was inevitable, but it brought the savage hurt of a knife thrust. He sat on the corner of a desk, looking at Wickford White. The Colonel was as sprucely dressed and vigorous-looking as ever; he had a frustrated look, too, as if his energy were kept from bursting bounds by some compulsion which he detested.

"Hallo, Rollison," he said. "Glad to see you again. 'Fraid this isn't working out as we hoped."

"Oh, come. Exactly as you hoped!"

"My dear chap! Violence in the Camp. More disappearances——"

"As Aird once said, when they felt themselves in danger they started to get nasty," Rollison pointed out. "Nothing we could do about it. They're badly worried."

He wondered if anyone could guess how worried he was. He looked at the stranger, recognized but couldn't place him. He was sturdily built, with good, regular features, rather pre-occupied. He gave a slight smile.

"My dear chap!" the Colonel exclaimed again. "Of course, you haven't met the Chief. Mr. Butlin—Mr. Rollison."

Now Rollison placed the stranger from his photographs. They shook hands, murmured politely.

"Go on, Wickford," Butlin said.

"Have to be frank," said Wickford White. "You haven't yet done what we hoped you'd do. Don't misunderstand me, I'm not complaining. But we hoped you would solve the problem quietly. Now we're getting disturbing reports from all over the Camp—the Campers are feeling jittery. Bad. Only the nervous ones so far, of course, but we're all very worried."

Rollison said : "I've told Wray—Uncle Pi—what to do about that." He explained what he'd planned.

"Astonishing!" exclaimed Wickford White. "That's exactly what Mr. Butlin suggested—get the Pied Piper ready."

"Nice to know I've done something right," Rollison said dryly.

"Don't misunderstand us," said Butlin, in a quiet voice. His smile was reassuring. "I've the fullest confidence in you, we all have, but when we heard of the murder of Susan Dell, we told the police everything—the terms on which we engaged you, our purpose, everything. But you represent us in the investigation. I'm sure the police will be glad of your help."

Rollison smiled. So he wasn't being politely fired.

"Nice of you. Thanks." Now there was Davies to deal with, the Yard to ask for help, the reassuring confidence of the Camp's owner.

"Hallo, here's Davies," Wickford White said.

Aird opened the door, and the Inspector came in briskly. He smiled all round, but nothing suggested that he had had much luck with Mrs. Beck or Beck himself.

"Well?" the Colonel burst out.

"Mrs. Beck says that she was walking in the gardens and was attacked from behind," said the Inspector, musically, "and that's all she can tell us, gentlemen." His voice went up and down, up and down. He looked at Rollison, and began to smile again, if faintly. "I'm glad to see you again, Mr. Rollison, I've been talking about you on the telephone with Scotland Yard."

"And I'm not arrested yet," Rollison marvelled.

Davies's smile broadened; his eyes crinkled.

"They've a high opinion of you," he said, as if he were pleasantly but very greatly surprised, "and they told me that you had asked them about this investigation, and also about the man Clark."

Butlin, the Colonel, Aird, and Llewellyn now had their turn to look startled.

"Just a precaution," Rollison said. "Never tread where the police don't want you to, unless you want to very badly."

Butlin smiled more broadly. "I knew we could rely on you not to take chances," he said. "I came just to tell you that. I have to be off. I'm overdue in London. Glad to leave you to look after our interests."

He shook hands all round, and went out with Aird.

Davies stroked his chin, as if to prevent himself from smiling.

"I think I see what you mean, now," he said. "They told me about this man Clark, and what he's been up to. I'm to pass the message on." He paused, not necessarily for effect; but he won effect. "They now know that he's still mixed up with a gang of jewel thieves."

No one spoke; until the Colonel exploded:

"*Jewels!*"

"Yes, Colonel White, stolen jewels," said Davies, his voice rising on the "els" until it was almost two notes higher than the "jew". "They aren't able to tell us much more about it, except that the woman Susan Dell was used as a decoy sometimes, she helped the thieves to keep the owners occupied while they took the jew*els*." He rubbed his nose again. "There's no telling until we have the inquest verdict, but I'll venture an opinion," went on Davies, so mildly that he might have been talking about the temperature of the water in the swimming-pool. "She didn't fall over those cliffs, indeed she didn't—she was pushed. There was a bruise on the back of her head and other marks which the police surgeon doesn't think are consistent with falling, and if he's right, then it would be a matter of murder, wouldn't it?"

"*Murder!*" exploded the Colonel; and Llewellyn gave a little popping echo of the word. "Murder! I must go and tell the Chief." He hurried to the door.

"Yes, indeed," said Davies, gravely. "Murder."

"Looking for Clark?" asked Rollison sharply.

"Didn't anyone tell you?" asked Davies, as if surprised; but he wasn't a fool, and probably knew quite well that no one else was aware of what had happened. "They found Clark's body, also—he was in the sea not so far away from here. His throat was cut."

No one spoke.

.   .   .   .

Rollison saw a picture in his mind's eye; of a crude crayon drawing of three Redcoats, one lying down and two sitting, each with a cut throat.

He could picture the flawless white perfection of Elizabeth Cherrell's throat.

Davies followed him to the door as he went away. Outside in the passage, the Inspector said:

"What will you do, Mr. Rollison?"

"I'm going to try Beck's wife," Rollison said. "She might change her mind. Why don't you station a man in the Sick Bay where she is—send him at once, by the back way. I'll go a long way round."

"Good idea, man," said Davies. "I'll send an officer at once."

Rollison walked across the Reception Hall. There was a milling crowd outside, and the Colonel appeared to be "protecting" his chief, who was beseiged by Campers and signing autograph books steadily.

"No, really, we *must* go!" the Colonel cried.

Rollison joined them, and they cleared a path, but were followed by a crowd. Butlin stopped by a children's playground, watching, smiling.

"You'll be late," the Colonel said plaintively.

"Ten minutes won't hurt," said Butlin, and turned to Rollison again. "I meant all I said, Mr. Rollison. Good-bye again."

As soon as he had gone, Rollison became the centre of attraction again. Many people looked at him, some openly, some furtively; there was whispering, and some Redcoats looked askance, too. The radio girl was saying something; that it was nearly dinner-time. Rollison had almost forgotten what it was like to feel hungry.

Jolly was in his chalet; a quiet Jolly, who listened and was obviously feeling subdued.

"More emphasis on jewels," he echoed, when Rollison finished.

"Yes. And now there's murder and the police involved, the pressure's on. Find out if the police are watching Beck, will you? He might try to skip."

He went to the drawer and took out the pencilled drawing. Jolly glanced at it.

"Any news of Uncle Pi?" Rollison asked abruptly.

"He was in Miss Cherrell's chalet for twenty minutes or so," Jolly said. "He appeared to have a key, but he may have borrowed a master-key from the maid. That is all, sir."

Rollison grunted, and left the chalet.

People were streaming towards the dining-halls, children were running; at least one in three looked back. He was going in a different direction from most of them. He reached the lower road and turned towards the Sick Bay—and as he reached a corner, Beck appeared.

He walked alongside Rollison.

Few Campers were about here; but two cars passed, and the passenger in one turned and looked back.

"Rollison," Beck said, at last; he spoke as if the act of using his voice hurt him, "don't say a word to the police about me. Not a word, do you understand. Or else——"

He crossed his throat with his finger. This time he didn't imitate the death rattle; that made it worse, because Rollison found himself waiting for the hideous sound.

"Nothing would stop it if I were arrested," Beck said. "Don't forget that."

He turned off the road; and a man in plain clothes followed him. This wasn't the moment to tackle Beck. But Beck was nervous. Had he attacked his own wife? Would he have done a crazy thing like that, knowing that it would bring in the police, and they would question, probably watch him?

Rollison walked on. He could feel the influence of the man, just as nearly everyone else who had anything to do with the affair seemed to feel it, but—was it justified? Were there others working with Beck who would murder? Was this an act? Almost a form of hypnosis?

Murder had been committed, hadn't it? Twice.

There was lovely Elizabeth with those glorious eyes and that fear—gone completely.

Was Beck bluffing?

Rollison could catch up with him, soon; could see him alone, but—he needed facts. He needed evidence to use against the man, evidence for which Elizabeth's safety might be bartered.

He reached the line of chalets which had a *First Aid* notice swinging above several. The Sister on duty said there was no reason why he shouldn't speak to Mrs. Beck—she was much better. The police had questioned her nearly an hour ago. She was extremely lucky, if that cord had been tied a little tighter . . .

Rosa lay on a bed; not in it. She wore a cotton dress of pale green with big, dark-green leaves. Her hair was drawn back from her forehead and looked like beaten brass. Her lipstick was smeared, and her powder had gone; her cheeks and nose were shiny.

When she saw Rollison, she started violently.

The Sister left them togeher.

"Well, Rosa," Rollison said, "why didn't you wait?"

She didn't look at him, seemed as if she wanted to be anywhere but in the same room.

"Go away," she breathed. "Go away!"

"It won't happen again, and——"

"Go *away!*"

"It won't——"

"It happened to Susan Dell!" she gasped. "She's disappeared, hasn't she? If it hadn't been for that, I wouldn't have——"

She stopped again.

"Tell me this, Rosa." Rollison pulled up a chair and sat by her side. He gave her a cigarette, and she seemed glad to draw on it. But she was reluctant to meet his eyes. "You want to save life, don't you?" Rollison persisted.

"Go—go away," she said sighingly.

"At least three, probably four people are in danger. You can help me—can't you?"

"I—I don't know anything."

"Rosa," he said, "you can tell me what you know. I'll make sure that nothing more happens to you. You needn't worry, you'll be quite safe."

She didn't speak.

"What can you tell me?"

"If—if he ever finds out——"

"He won't until it's too late," Rollison said. He watched her closely. He saw that she was looking now at him and now at the window—as if she felt the presence of her husband and believed that in a moment he would be glaring in here with those searing eyes. "Where are the men, Rosa? Where's Elizabeth Cherrell?"

"I—I don't know about the girl," she whispered. "I heard Cy say something, not—not much." She clutched Rollison's hand and pulled herself up. He saw the redness at her throat; as it had been at Middleton's. "But the men—Rollison, if I tell you, don't let Cy——"

"He won't hurt you."

"You don't know him!"

"He won't hurt you any more," Rollison said soothingly. "I'll see to it. I'll see that you're guarded, day and night, from this moment on."

She dropped back on her pillows.

"They're in some caves in the rocks, near Harlech," she said. "You get from here by boat. The men were kept in an old barn up by the Camp stables until after dark, then taken away."

"Why does he do it? What have they found out?"

"I don't know," she gasped, "I don't——"

Then she screamed and covered her face with her hands; and fell back as if she were dead.

Rollison swung round towards the window, in time to see the dark, wiry hair of Cyrus Beck as the man moved away.

CHAPTER XIX

TALK OF JEWELS

THE Sister came hurrying in as Rollison turned from the window. Rosa lay absolutely still. Rollison watched the nurse bending over her, calling her, slapping her face lightly. Rosa seemed to have gone into a trance. Her eyes were open, and she stared at the ceiling but made no response.

Rollison remembered his earlier, uneasy thought—that Beck's influence was almost hypnotic. He could induce fear. He could induce shock symptoms.

Could he?

Rollison went into the dispensing room, where another nurse was mixing bright liquids. There were stacks of bandages, enamel trays, surgical instruments, all the paraphernalia of the first-aid room. Davies's man stood up from behind the door, tapping his notebook.

"All right?" asked Rollison, mildly.

"*Now* we've got 'em, sir!" The man was bright-eyed and eager to be off.

"I hope so," Rollison said.

"We will get some of the fishermen who know every cave in the rocks," said Davies's man, "they won't get them away now, take it from me."

He hurried off.

Rollison went back into the sick-room. Rosa still lay on her back, eyes wide open and staring towards the ceiling. The Sister had piled clothes on her.

"She seems all right," she said. "Pulse is a bit fast, and her respiration's a bit shallow, that's all. Just shock, but I'd better fetch the doctor again."

"Yes," Rollison said. "Wasn't her pulse fast when she first came here?"

"Not *very*." The Sister gave a funny little laugh. "If that cord had been tied a little tighter, I don't think we could have saved her."

"Moral to murderers, never do a job in too much of a hurry," Rollison said. "Nothing I can do?"

"I don't think so."

Rollison stood at the foot of the bed, looking down at Rosa. There was no way of telling whether she recognized him or not; she lay absolutely comatose. Now and again she blinked; that was all.

He went out.

Time had passed without his realizing it. Dusk was falling. In the west the sun seemed to be sinking into the sea, a fiery red ball at which he could look with comfort through the haze. In another direction he could make out the shore— and, if he concentrated, Harlech Castle and the rocky cliffs below it.

As he entered the large reception room, the middle-aged woman with the grey hair and the nice wrinkles came across to him; she looked as if she had been lying in wait. She wore navy blue and white, was very simply and very neatly dressed; she looked charming. If there had to be a woman in Jolly's life, she looked right. Her eyes smiled, although there was a serious glint in them.

"Excuse me, sir, but Mr. Jolly is worried because you haven't had any dinner."

"I'll get a snack, thanks."

"He asked me to tell you that he has put one in your chalet," she added. "And also—*they* have arrived." She changed the direction of her gaze.

Rollison looked in the same direction. Leaning against the counter beneath the big sign KEYS was a large man—a man of the size and, if the truth be told, much the appearance of the burly, brutish Rickett. But there was nothing brutish about this giant, in spite of his large paunch, his blunted features, and his two superb cauliflower ears.

He had smallish, pale-blue eyes; he winked.

Rollison winked back.

"Jolly suggests that the best place for you and Mr. Ebbutt to meet might be in the Church of England building, next to the bicycle store," the nice woman went on, smiling again. "It's always open. Mr. Ebbutt will be there at ten o'clock."

"Tell him fine," Rollison praised her.

"Thank you so much." She smiled as if she really meant that. "Jolly himself will be at the chalet," she added.

"Will you keep him company?"

"I'm just going on duty."

"Sad for Jolly," Rollison said, and managed to grin without having to force it.

He felt perkier. Ebbutt was a monumental tower of strength, and still possessed that terrific and devastating punch. He had three men with him. If, as Rollison now felt convinced, things were not altogether what they seemed, it would be possible to take some action without relying on the police.

Davies was in Aird's office, with Aird and the Colonel. Llewellyn wasn't there. On the desk was a tray, glasses, whisky and soda, gin and vermouth.

"What will you have?" asked the Colonel, and Aird moved, to pour out.

"Whisky-and-splash, please."

"Cigarette?" said the Colonel, and thrust out his case.

"Thanks."

"Congratulations," said the Colonel, as if he meant it. He flicked his lighter. "Light?" He paused. "If it weren't for you, we shouldn't have got anything like as far as this. Understand your reputation now—not afraid to work with the police when necessary!"

Davies was looking steadily at Rollison.

Aird held out a glass.

"Ah, thanks," said Rollison. "Damnation to all murderers and handcuffs to all crooks." He drank; he drank again. "That's *good*." He drank, and Aird hovered hospitably near. "May I?" Rollison beamed. "I feel as if I haven't had a drop for an age," he went on, and dropped on to the arm of a chair. "What's doing, Inspector?"

"I've telephoned to Harlech," Davies said, "and my men are on the way to help, now, by sea. Within an hour, men who know that coast as they know the palms of their hands will be searching."

"Just a risk——" the Colonel began, and stopped; as if he were reluctant to go on.

"That they might have been moved," said Davies. "And although the woman has implicated her husband, it doesn't prove anything."

"Holding Beck?"

"Not yet," said Davies, "unless you can give us evidence."

Rollison could—but once Beck were in a charge-room he would be right out of reach; and that wouldn't do.

"Would a man attack his own wife like that?" Rollison asked.

"Well, would he, now?" Davies was perplexed. "I don't know. But I'm having him watched, and the man Rickett, also."

"Middleton?"

"Yes," Davies said. He did not seem to be really pleased with life. "But if they want to leave the Camp, we can't very well keep them here, can we?"

Rollison shrugged.

"What we can do is to search Miss Cherrell's chalet," Davies said. "Like to be present when we do?"

"I would," Rollison said, and glanced at his watch. It was twenty minutes to ten. "But I'm famished, and there's a snack in my chalet. Shouldn't think you'll find any caves still occupied," he added.

"I'll let you know," Davies promised.

Jolly was in Rollison's chalet. The "little snack" was a cold collation of generous proportions. There was also beer and, for consolation afterwards, whisky-and-soda.

A subdued Jolly watched Rollison eat and listened to everything that had happened and all that he didn't know. It was quite a story.

"Now put a finger on the weak spots," Rollison invited.

Jolly considered.

"This peculiar *influence* of the man Beck," he said at last. "It is greatly exaggerated, I think. It is obviously true that he can frighten people, but hypnotic—I wouldn't say that, sir. I think he has set out to create exactly that impression."

"And succeeded."

"Too well, I imagine," said Jolly.

"Probably." Rollison speared a piece of tomato. "Next?"

Jolly didn't answer immediately. He studied Rollison, his eyes slightly narrowed and very thoughtful. He began to smile. There was no doubt that the holiday atmosphere or the woman with the nice wrinkles had made a great difference to Jolly.

"Will you forgive me, sir, for asking what has happened to make you lighter-hearted?" He almost purred.

"Wrong," Rollison said. "Until we get Elizabeth Cherrell free, I'm a man of Stygian gloom."

But he wasn't.

There was something new, brighter, in his mood. He felt, if not light-hearted, then at least past the worst of the black depression. He no longer felt that the odds were hopelessly against him.

"I can't imagine that Ebbutt's arrival alone would be quite so refreshing," said Jolly dryly.

"Call it that. Or say that I'm soon going to fire a broadside at Cy Beck. There's a flaw in Beck's campaign. A big one. He hopes I won't see it."

"If you say there is I am fully prepared to agree," conceded Jolly, "but——" He shrugged. "I confess that I haven't seen it yet. Do you mean that he will have assumed that his wife made some kind of statement, and that he will move the missing men, perhaps Elizabeth Cherrell also, from the caves?"

"No."

Jolly shrugged again.

"Work at it," Rollison urged. "It's much better if two of us reach the same conclusion. I'll bet all Butlin's to a Bournemouth boarding-house that the police don't find anyone in any cave near Harlech." He obviously delighted in being mysterious as he stood up. "I'm going to see Ebbutt at the Church of England building."

Before he reached the door, there was a tap.

"Allow me," said Jolly, and went forward swiftly.

Rollison felt quite sure that he half-expected trouble. Instead, there was a policeman in uniform, a large and stolid man; in the quiet light outside half a dozen Campers stood about.

"Mr. Rollison, please," the constable said.

"I'm Rollison."

"Inspector Davies's compliments, and would you be good enough to come with me to Miss Cherrell's chalet?"

"Oh," said Rollison. "Yes."

He went out. He know that he could rely on Jolly telling Ebbutt that he had been delayed. With the constable, he walked the few hundred yards to the girl's chalet—and they were followed by at least a dozen people and by silence. Everywhere the atmosphere was uneasy.

A crowd outside Elizabeth's chalet was silent and watchful, too. Several policemen stood about. Then Uncle Pi and Middleton showed up, kept away from the chalet door by a policeman. Middleton was talking in a low-pitched, angry voice:

"It's absolutely crazy. Madness! She wouldn't——"

He didn't finish.

Uncle Pi's eyes had a glow in them; there was also hostility when he looked at Middleton and, for that matter, when he looked at Rollison. He didn't smile.

"What's that?" Rollison asked.

"The police have found stolen jewels in Liz's chalet," Uncle Pi said. "Middleton has another crazy idea. He thinks you put them there."

CHAPTER XX

SEARCH BY NIGHT

DAVIES and two others were in the chalet. It looked quite tidy. The bed had been moved away from the wall, and there were some chippings of cement on the floor; one of the men had dusty clothes.

On the small dressing-chest was a little heap of jewels.

They scintillated brilliantly as Rollison stepped inside. The police still held Uncle Pi and Middleton back; Middleton forcibly. Inspector Davies, his hat on the back of his head, smoothed down his silvery hair and spared Rollison a preoccupied smile.

"Didn't you find these when you searched this chalet?" he asked.

That showed the cunning of a skilled hand.

"Would I search anyone's chalet?" asked Rollison, blank-faced.

Davies smiled, almost dreamily.

Rollison had searched, even if he were not going to admit it to the police; and he had moved the bed out and seen nothing on the floor which might suggest a hiding-place.

This had been done since.

"How did you find it?"

"Obviously a new patch of cement," Davies said, "and the jewels were in a box under it." He smoothed down his hair again. "I can be sure that one or two of them are stolen, for certain," he added. "I recognize them from Scotland Yard circulars. I expect the others will be identified, also."

Rollison said : "I wouldn't be surprised."

He studied the jewels. Most of them had been taken out of their settings, but some had not. There were diamonds, rubies, sapphires, and emeralds; some gems were large, by normal standards, huge. Staring at precious stones had a curious effect on him; they seemed to fascinate. The size of this haul did. He liked to be conservative in estimating such things, but would be astonished if the total value of the jewellery was less than ten thousand pounds.

It looked so clear, now; smuggling precious stones out of the country, selling them for dollars.

Davies said: "I'm going to have each one tested for finger-prints, mind you, we can't take them away yet."

"No," said Rollison. "You can't."

Then the muttering from Middleton grew into a shout. There was a scuffle, and he rushed forward. His eyes were wild, he looked like a man demented.

"Liz wouldn't know anything about it, this is a foul trick to frame her. It must be!" He glared at Davies. "If you think Miss *Cherrell* had anything to do with this, you're mad. Why don't you ask *Rollison* what he knows?"

"Now, come! The last time we were talking you thought that——"

"Oh, you're all the same," cried Middleton. "Police and private detectives are as thick as thieves. I'm sick to death of the lot of you, but—find *Liz*. Understand?" He almost choked. "Find Liz, or they'll kill her."

People were listening outside.

There was Uncle Pi.

He came in, quietly.

"Dry up, Dick," he said in his calmest voice. "You ought to know better than to start shouting the odds about murder in the Camp, it will only put the wind up Campers without doing any good. Let's get along."

"They've got to find Liz!"

"They'll find her," Uncle Pi soothed. "Come on." He slid his arm through Middleton's, and led the way out.

Rollison half-expected Davies to stop them, but he didn't. Rollison watched Uncle Pi's shoulders, hunched beneath that red coat; and remembered that he had been in Elizabeth's chalet; he could have planted those jewels.

Anyone could have planted them.

The sure thing was that they had not been there that

morning. Whoever had hidden them had used quick-drying cement. It might have been Liz; there was no certainty. Liz could be a party to these crimes, might have been spirited away because she was suspect and might lead Rollison or the police to the truth.

Davies said: "What would be the point of framing her and kidnapping her at the same time?" He smoothed down his hair, and seemed to be talking more to himself than to anyone in the chalet. "Isn't it much more likely that she knew these were here, and was so frightened that she made off?"

"Much more," Rollison agreed. "Logically."

Davies looked at him. "What *do* you think?"

Only the police were within earshot; there were two or three dozen people outside now, looking in; unless he raised his voice, they wouldn't hear him.

"I think this is part of a magnificent bluff," he said. "A gem of a bluff! I think we're supposed to be spending all our time worrying about Liz when something or someone else is much more important. I think"—he smiled beautifully—"that you ought to take your men off Cyrus Beck and Rickett, and leave them to me. You won't, of course."

"Why should I?"

"While they're followed by the police, they won't do a thing. If they think the police have lost interest in them, they might."

"What would they do?"

"I'm not clairvoyant," Rollison protested. "I'm suggesting that these jewels have been planted here to blind us to the real game. That we've been shown the finger pointing this way, and it's the wrong way. I think there must be much more than this packet of jewels."

"They must be worth at least ten thousand pounds," Davies reasoned.

"Some sprat," Rollison agreed. He gave the smooth smile which Jolly had noticed; the same gleam was in his eyes. "I think I'm beginning to see what's on, Inspector."

"So do I," said Davies, warmly. "Do a little mental arithmetic about jewel robberies in the past few months. Start with the Minchester House affair in London, with twenty-five thousand pounds worth; add the Manchester one, the Bond Street robbery, the country house burglary in Leicestershire, and the big job at Knyton Hall, in Kent. They all topped twenty thousand pounds, didn't they now? That's a hundred thousand, and worth a few risks for any man. Remember that it's the work of a gang, and we have only mentioned the big jobs—there have been dozens more little ones. Say *two* hundred thousand pounds, man! It would be worth losing ten thousand pounds worth or so to give them time to take the rest to safety, wouldn't it?"

"There would indeed," murmured the Toff.

"See that rose-coloured diamond with the broken claw setting?" Davies asked. "It's part of the Knyton Hall robbery—there's a picture of it in the *Police Gazette*. They made a mistake, leaving it in the setting, but they were so sure of themselves, weren't they?" He gave a little crow of a laugh.

"So very sure. Will you take your men off Beck?" asked Rollison.

"He *must* be watched," Davies said emphatically. "I don't want to be unhelpful, but——"

"I've some friends here who can replace them," Rollison declared. "Good chaps, too."

"Ah, but we can see what's happening now," said Davies, greatly excited. "The jewels from these robberies are brought up here for disposal—for handing over by the thieves to the fences, the buyers. It has probably been happening all the season. People staying at the Camp can bring in guests, in early and late seasons there are a lot of week-enders. To keep the flow running smoothly, the gang would need one man here all the time; at least one. That could be a Camper or a Redcoat—we'll find out soon now. Every now and again, negotiations are necessary, and Beck or whoever is Boss comes here to do it. This time, they were really important negotiations—and things went wrong when you were asked to look round."

He stopped, and waited as if for approval; even congratulation. Rollison did not have the heart to express doubts.

"Could be," he said. "We'll see. Be a friend, Davies, let me have a little chat with Cy Beck, without being followed or watched."

Davies had obvious doubts; but agreed.

.   .   .   .

Cy Beck was in his chalet. Rickett and another man whom Rollison couldn't see clearly, were just outside. Beck looked more than ever like an Old Testament prophet—except for the viciousness which lived in his eyes.

"What do you want?" His voice was gruff; he was nervous, and the Toff loved dealing with nervous bad men.

"Just a little chat, Cy," he said. "About caves in cliffs and aeroplanes and dollar bills and things."

Beck caught his breath.

"Don't say that stung," said Rollison, as if startled. "My dear Cy, I know a lot more than that, and guess much more. The police would clap you in a cold, cruel cell on suspicion the moment I told them about those dollar bills, too. But I'm less interested in currency frauds than in Liz Cherrell and the three Redcoats. I want them here. Quick. Say by tomorrow morning. If they don't turn up——"

He didn't finish, but waved brightly at Beck, went out, ignored Rickett and the other man, and whistled as he walked away.

Beck would have to act fast, now; and with luck would make serious mistakes.

He wasn't followed.

He went back to Elizabeth's hut; Davies was still there, but before he spoke, Rollison saw a woman, hurrying along. She pushed past a policeman, but he caught her arm.

"Mr. Rollison!" she called.

It was Jolly's girl-friend with the nicely lined face, but her charming expression had gone. She was touched with the

Thing which had touched so many people here: fear. It showed in her eyes, her expression, her tension.

"Sorry," Rollison said to Davies. "Hallo?" He didn't know her name.

"May I speak to you, please—urgently." She glanced at Davies. She seemed to be trying to pass on a message of great urgency—and that fear was in her. What should she fear, unless it were something to do with Jolly? "Confidentially, *please*. It's desperately urgent," the woman added. "Please don't waste another word."

Jolly might have said that; and in the circumstances he would have meant: "Please don't *say* another word." The woman was straining against the barrier of the policeman's arm. "Please, please, please understand," she seemed to plead.

Rollison hurried out to her, and the policeman lowered his arm.

"Trouble for Jolly?" asked Rollison sharply.

"Yes."

So this was Beck's answer; and it could be deadly.

"All right." Rollison turned to Davies, heart thudding. "I'll be seeing you. Soon."

He took the woman's elbow, and hustled her through the crowd. It had become very thick; dozens were here. Most of the people were middle-aged, but some were youngsters— only the youngsters seemed to find a thrill in this. The rest looked worried; anxious. There were the whispers, the rumours: a murderer, a killer was at large. There loomed the threat of panic, an intangible thing it was hard to beat. Uncle Pi had tried, and Middleton had undone everything he had attempted. From Middleton's wild words rumour would have spread fast—would now be carried to the dance halls, the theatres, the games rooms, the bars.

Two or three youths followed them.

Rollison still held the woman's arm. They were on a path leading towards the offices and the main buildings.

"What is it?"

"They've—kidnapped *him*."

It wasn't a surprise, now; it wasn't even a shock. He had sensed it from the moment he had seen her expression. He felt curiously flat; cool; determined. Here was something which could bring unparalleled disaster. Twenty-one years of service, loyalty, counsel, and friendship were vital things; they had great depth and significance. If one individual in the whole world mattered more to Rollison than any others, it was Jolly. He was part of life; it was unthinkable that he should need help and it should not be given.

And Rollison could blame himself for dallying too long, leaving Beck alone too long. Beck had believed himself to be in the ascendency; now he was.

"How?" Rollison asked abruptly.

"He'd had an idea, and wanted to ask me something about it. He telephoned and said he was coming. He didn't arrive. I was getting worried when a man——"

"Beck?"

"No."

"Who?"

"I've never noticed him before. Just a man—rather young, hard-looking." Her voice was unsteady. "He said that Jolly wouldn't be coming back until you'd had another talk with Beck."

Rollison said : "Where?"

"Beck will tell you."

"So he gives orders." Rollison lit a cigarette—then thought to offer her one. She wouldn't smoke. "What was Jolly's idea?"

"He didn't say much—he didn't want to, on the telephone. He asked me for time-tables of any regular service out of the Camp passing the spot where—where all three disappeared. I was getting them ready——"

"Is it easy?"

"Fairly, there aren't many regular services."

"Only one that matters," Rollison said.

They were outside the offices, now. He knew that many more people had followed them; including policemen. He knew that Davies wasn't satisfied.

Until he knew what Beck wanted, Rollison wasn't going to do any deal with Davies, with anyone.

In the big reception hall a youngish, shortish man, with sparse black hair brushed straight back from his forehead, thin features, and a nasty thin mouth, sat near the desk. He grinned crookedly at Rollison.

"That's him," the woman said. "Do *you* know what Jolly——"

"I've an idea."

"What?"

"I'll keep it to myself," Rollison told her. He felt her take his arm, as if appealingly. She was fifty, perhaps fifty-five; but she had a charm which was given to few women, and was so very nice to look at. "No," he said, "that doesn't mean that I don't trust you. It simply means that I can't take the risk of you knowing. You might disappear, too."

"That's right," said the man.

He stood up, and sauntered towards Rollison. He was insolent—his movements, the twist of his lips, everything was a calculated insult.

"Beck wants you," he said.

"Where?"

"Viennese Ballroom."

"When?"

"Now."

"I've a job to do first," Rollison said. "I'll be ten minutes or so." He turned to the woman, and gripped her hands. "Stay within sight of other people all the time. Don't take any chances."

"I—won't." She had fine eyes; they could be radiant. "Save him, won't you," she said. "He——"

She didn't finish.

The hard man sneered.

Rollison went out of the Reception Hall, with Beck's man on his heels.

F

CHAPTER XXI

SAVE JOLLY

OUTSIDE, the man from Beck followed him. There were few people about; but there would soon be more when the theatres would be emptied and the bars closed. In the distance, Rollison heard the booming of a drum; then someone began to sing, near by.

> *"Will you please put a penny on the drum,*
> *Will you please put a penny on the drum,*
> *We only want a tanner*
> *To buy a new piano,*
> *So please put a penny on the drum."*

Just a nonsense doggerel; nightly, highly-spirited nonsense.

Others took it up; in the distance drums were beating time. One drew near. Round the corner came a Redcoat beating a drum, and behind him a laughing crocodile of people, mostly young, clinging to one another, shouting, singing :

> *"Come and join us, come and join us,*
> *Come and join our happy party.*
> *Come and join us, come and join us,*
> *Come and join our happy throng."*

They marched past, noisy, swift.

Other drums were leading other crocodiles towards the main ballroom, where they would all converge.

The hard man, close to Rollison, said : "Only your man Jolly isn't so happy. Don't waste any time. When Beck sends for a man, he wants him *quick*."

> *"Will you please put a penny on the drum . . ."*

"*Boom, boom, boom, boom,*" went the drums.

"So forget where you were going," the hard-faced man said.

Rollison had to lose him; had to see Ebbutt first. Ebbutt might still be waiting at the church; he was patient by nature, and he had faith. The crocodile was nearly past, but others were coming—all heading fast towards the Viennese Ballroom.

"Soon," Rollison said.

He joined a crocodile. A plump girl was just in front of him, holding the waist of the man ahead; a man behind gripped Rollison's waist, Beck's envoy was squeezed out. They went on wildly, surging, as they would in the *Conga*.

> *"Boom, boom, boom, boom!*
> *Come and join us, come and join us,*
> *Come and join . . ."*

They turned a corner, and Beck's man wasn't in sight. Rollison slipped away, and the girl cried: "Oh, spoil sport!" He ran ahead of the crocodile, and in front of the Redcoat who was beating the drum at the head of it. Beck's man didn't show up. A huge crowd had gathered near the entrance to the Ballroom, and some of the crocodiles were already inside. The ballroom would soon be a swarming mass, all fears and uncertainty forgotten in the wild exhilaration of the nightly ceremony.

> *"Come and join our happy throng!"*

Only Jolly wasn't so happy.

Rollison didn't run; too many people were coming towards the ballroom, in his way. But he bored a way through, elbowing some, jostling others. He would be able to pick out the hard-faced man if he saw him; he didn't see him.

Beck might have others here.

This was big. That had been clear from the beginning; big; worth taking desperate risks for; worth murder, if you were of the type who could kill without remorse or compunction. Was Davies right?

> *". . . our happy throng."*

Jolly, three missing Redcoats, and Elizabeth Cherrell weren't very happy. He felt happier about Liz. Had she known about those buried jewels, her chalet would have been too obvious a hiding-place.

The drumbeats stopped; the singing and the shouting died.

Few people were about when Rollison reached the church. Outside, the only indication that it was a church was the arched doorway, and the notice-boards outside. Light shone inside. He went in. Here were the pews, there was the altar, facing him; and candles on it; and dim lighting. There was the cross. There, standing against the wall, was Ebbutt—the massive Ebbutt. Chewing. He looked bored to distraction until he saw Rollison, then he beamed. His red, rosy face could light up marvellously.

"Why, Mr. Ar, fought you was never comin'." His voice was muted.

"Sorry, Bill, I——"

"Gotta story to tell my ole gel," beamed Ebbutt with child-like delight. "I bet she never expected me to 'ang arahnd inside a church for over a 'nour, up 'ere at Butlin's. 'You keep away from those young hussies up there, and as soon's Mr. Ar's finish wiv' yer, you come back,' she said. Them's 'er orders! S'fact. Still trying ta make me join the Harmy, she is. I suppose it's okay for those as like it, but I never did like brass bands. I——"

He stopped.

His voice had been low-pitched all the time, as if in a kind of intuitive reverence. He was bursting with words because of his boredom; and in his way he was looking forward to telling his Salvation Army wife a thing she would find it hard to believe. But now he saw the look in Rollison's eyes, and his voice tapered off.

"Bill," Rollison said, "there's been a lot of kidnapping. Three officials from here, a girl, and now Jolly. And some murder."

"*Jolly,*" breathed Ebbutt.

Those who knew him and Jolly also knew that when they

had first met they had disliked each other with the fierce antipathy of extreme opposites. The one thing they had in common was devotion to the Toff, and even that had been for different reasons. But the years had mellowed them—and now, Ebbutt's little pale-blue eyes showed shock and alarm at the news.

"Yes, Bill. Listen. I'm going to the Viennese Ballroom, and want you to follow me. I'll touch at least two people, perhaps three, with my fingers—this way." He put the first two fingers of his right hand together, and tapped Ebbutt on the shoulder with them. "See that?"

"Okay."

"Follow them," Rollison said. "Have all your boys with you, to follow the men I touch. You, yourself, follow me." He demonstrated again. "Don't waste any time, but send for the police. You'll find them at the offices."

"Okeydoke," Bill said.

"And if I vanish," Rollison said, "don't lose any time either. Tell the police to get to the aerodrome in a hurry. It's so near Ireland it's perfect for smuggling. There's a lot of traffic, some charter flying, nothing likely to cause suspicion. Say I'm almost certainly on it or near it, and the police must stop any plane taking off. I——"

He stopped.

He heard the droning of an aeroplane high in the star-decked sky. It wasn't unusual. It might not be one of the *See the Camp by Night* flights; but probably it was.

Jolly might be up there.

He and Jolly had seen all the available evidence and added it together and come to the same conclusion. One easy way to get the Redcoats and anyone out of the Camp was through the regular "free transport" to the airport. The one thing which would hardly be noticed leaving was that old Army truck which did its journey a dozen times a day. The easy way to make people vanish into thin air was to take them up in the air.

And *drop* them?

"Okay," Ebbutt said. "Gimme five minutes to line up the

ovvers, Mr. Ar. Brought five, arter all—couple more couldn't resist a bit of a spree at Billy B's." He winked as he crept out of the church door. "They're in the cycle store. I'll tell yer when it's okay."

.   .   .   .   .

It was quiet in the church. Rollison's mind was not quiet, yet he seemed to gain confidence here.

.   .   .

The engine of the aeroplane droned high above his head as Rollison walked towards the ballroom.

Crowds of people were gathered outside, bright lights shone, the steady beat of the dance band came faintly.

Behind Rollison was Ebbutt; and behind Ebbutt, the five men who had come with him from the East End of London. They owed the Toff much; he owed them plenty, too. But he wasn't thinking of them. He was thinking of the aeroplane and the probability that the missing men and others had been taken out of the district in a 'plane. He was thinking of Susan Dell's bashed and battered body—dropped from a height, remember. He was thinking of a crude drawing and red throats—and the news that Clark had been found with his throat cut.

He was thinking of Elizabeth Cherrell's fears; and Rosa Beck's fears—and of Cyrus Beck, with those piercing dark eyes and the influence which they seemed to hold.

He went into the ballroom.

The hard-faced man, standing just inside, straightened up as Rollison appeared. He looked past Rollison, obviously expecting to see the police; fear changed to puzzlement. He drew nearer. Pushed against him by the crowd, Rollison laid two fingers on his shoulder; that made him a marked man.

"Where've you been?"

"Trying to forget you."

"If you've told the police——"

"My poor fool, I don't need any help from the police." Rollison beamed.

The man led the way round the walls of the ballroom. At one point they were raised in four tiers, rising up from the dance floor. Hundreds of Campers, mostly the middle-aged and elderly ones, sat on brightly painted chairs and watched the dancing. At any other time Rollison would have been awed by the sight. The huge floor was crammed so tightly with people that there wasn't a spare inch of space. Two thousand people must have been on it. The band, on its raised dais, was playing a Square dance; a caller was yelling his head off through the microphone.

> *"Honour your partners,*
> *Honour your corners,*
> *Set your square and here we go.*
> *Ladies to the centre . . ."*

The dancers were following his instructions, everyone was moving at the same moment. The seething mass was like the waves of a tumultuous sea. On nearly every face was a set smile. Those who did not know the calling and the steps tried to follow; those who knew tried to guide willing or giggling partners.

The hard-faced man led Rollison towards another door, near a licensed bar.

Beck sat against the ballroom wall, with Rickett on one side of him and Rickett's loose-mouthed wife on the other side. Crowding the bar doorway to watch the dancing were Campers and Redcoats—at least a dozen Redcoats, men and women. They saw Rollison, and nudged one another. Some Campers saw him, too, and the mood of unease touched them all.

Rickett stood up.

Rollison touched him.

Ebbutt and his men, apparently part of a flowing tide of people, walked along the gangways between rows of chairs, and saw that. They also saw Rollison stumble, touch Beck and the woman, then recover.

"Sorry," he said, poker-faced.

"I'd like to —— you," Rickett's wife said viciously.

"Be quiet," Beck told her. "Sit down," he said to Rollison.

Rollison sat down in the chair which Rickett had left vacant. Rickett didn't go far away; he pretended to watch the dancing.

> "*Ladies to the centre, back to the Bar,*
> *Gents to the centre with a right-hand star.*"

"Listen," Beck said, "I've got Jolly, I've got the girl, I've got the other three. They're alive. They don't have to stay that way. Take it from me, if I don't leave this camp the way I want to, they won't stay alive. I'm working with others. They've killed twice, and they'll kill again if necessary. Don't make any mistake about that."

Rollison said: "So what?"

"You keep away from the police," Beck ordered flatly. "See? Keep right away from them."

Rollison said: "I can't keep them away from you."

"You'd better try," Beck growled. "And listen—you'd better talk. What do you know about dollars?"

Rollison didn't answer.

"You'll talk," Beck said, "or else——"

He didn't finish; but he told Rollison one thing, clearly; he was still nervous.

The dancing was going on wildly, men and women were kicking out, prancing, whirling, sweating, gasping; and the caller bellowed and the music boomed, and Beck's voice was like venom in Rollison's ear, audible because it was so close:

"You've got to talk to me *and* hold the police off, or Jolly and all the others——"

Beck didn't make the gesture of cutting his throat; he did mimic a death rattle. It sounded above the music, the thud of feet, the hoarse calling over the microphone.

The dance was nearing its climax; dancers looked frenzied and near the point of exhaustion.

"See," Beck said. "I've other legmen here. If anything goes wrong, that's it and all about it. Not one of the five prisoners will live. You're going to stall the police and come with me—and talk."

Yes, he was jittery. He wanted to get away and was frightened in case the police should stop him. He could be followed; he had to be. He and his men would recognize the police, but wouldn't guess that Ebbutt and the East Enders were after them.

Then Beck looked away—and stiffened.

CHAPTER XXII

POLICE CORDON

THE police stood at the door.

When he looked across the ballroom through the grey mist of smoke, Rollison saw more uniformed figures at each door. Davies wasn't in sight, but he probably wasn't far away.

"He said he didn't talk to the dicks," the messenger muttered, leaning forward, "he said——"

"Shut up, Jake." Beck's voice sizzled.

"I didn't," Rollison said. "Police are funny people. They do what they like." But now they could kill all hope.

"This time they don't," said Beck. "If they come and get me, they'll wish they hadn't, and so will you. Okay, Jake," he said, "get going. You wait, Rollison."

Jake moved away, swiftly.

The dance was still on, the caller was yelling, men and women were flinging themselves about with such wild abandon that collapse seemed only seconds away. One of Ebbutt's men, a tall and melancholy looking Cockney wearing a brown jacket, went after Jake. Two others were in the bar doorway, two behind Ebbutt near one of the square pillars and watching the fantastic scene.

The police didn't move.

Davies appeared with a sergeant, and made his way slowly towards Rollison and Beck. Beck's tension showed. One boney hand clutched his knee; the fingers of the other tightened on Rollison's left wrist.

"Tell Davies to lay off," he said. "If he doesn't, I'll start so much trouble he'll wish he'd never been born. I'll turn this crowd into a panic-stricken mob. A couple of shots, a couple of slashes with a knife, and a bit of shouting—don't make any mistake, Rollison. Jake's gone to give the signal— if it's needed."

He stared at Davies. And there wasn't much he hadn't planned.

"And you can say good-bye to Jolly," he added.

There might be a touch of madness in him, but above everything else, he knew he could do what he threatened. He had always been convinced that he could get away with his crimes; had planned each move with a master's touch.

Why?

"And when the crowd's panicked," he went on. "I'll get away. Once get that mob stampeding, and it would take a regiment to control the Camp. You know it. Keep Davies away from me. Go on."

Rollison stood up.

He pushed past Ebbutt, who didn't glance at him. There was Jolly to save; Liz; and the unknown men. What could he do?—what should he do if Davies were coming to get Beck?

The music stopped.

A wild cheer roared out from the watchers and dancers together. The swarming mass went still. It seemed as if two thousand people gasped gustily for breath at the identical moment, and then everyone began to surge away from the floor at once. They packed the doorways; it was impossible to keep them back. The police could do nothing in the crush.

Davies reached Rollison.

"We're going to hold Beck," he said.

"Why?"

"Two of his wife's rings are stolen goods," said Davies. "Now we know that, we can't wait any longer."

Rollison said slowly: "He's made two threats—to kill the prisoners and to panic the crowd, if you don't let him go."

Davies caught his breath as that sank in.

"*What?*" breathed the sergeant behind him.

"And I think he'll do it," Rollison went on.

Davies looked towards Beck. Rollison couldn't see the man, because he had his back towards him. But Rickett was very near, straining his ears to catch the policeman's word.

The crowd had advanced from the floor towards the tiers, and were flooding along the passages, taking every chair that was free, sitting on one another's knees, fanning themselves, gasping for breath.

The band started to play again, this time a quickstep.

"We can't—let them *blackmail* us," Davies said in a toneless voice.

"If he panics this crowd, what's going to happen next?" asked Rollison. "Half a dozen people might be trampled to death. More. It's a bad risk."

"He *can't* be allowed to blackmail the police!"

"Listen," Rollison reasoned. "See that big man there—with the yellow pullover—don't nod."

"Yes," Davies said.

"Tell him to take his friends to the airfield—to get there through the fences and not along the road, then watch for developments. Tell him I'll probably be there soon, as Beck's prisoner. Understand?"

"We can't——"

"If Beck stampedes this crowd he can get away," Rollison said reasonably. "I know what you feel like, but you'll get him sooner or later. Waiting a bit now should save trouble here, and give me a chance to save Jolly and the others."

"Your man?"

"Yes, gone with the rest."

Davies said through his clenched teeth: "My duty's plain enough, Mr. Rollison. I've reason to believe that the man is a dangerous criminal, and I must——"

Across his words, across the brisk music, across the scuffling feet and the babble of voices, there came a short, sharp explosion; and a flash. Everything stopped; even the band. Into the empty silence, there came a scream—short, sharp, piercing.

Others followed from different parts of the ballroom. By Rollison, Rickett's wife stood up and screamed as if she couldn't stop, loose mouth wide open, hands beating at her breast. The band started up again, but another explosion came before the music drowned the screaming.

The second explosion came from the band dais.

The men and girls in the band seemed to split up, to sway and fall in different directions. A saxophone and a trumpet went up into the air, then crashed. A girl fell off the platform. The pianist jumped up, then dropped down; and all her weight went on the keys, making a hideous cacaphony.

Lights started to go out.

Blackness added to terror.

Men rushed about wildly. Davies was pushed in the back, his sergeant stumbled, Rollison felt his legs hooked from under him. He kept his balance. The rushing crowd carried him helplessly towards the door. People were calling out to friends or screaming.

"Let me out!"

"Dolly, where are you?"

"Let's get out!"

"Ted—Ted!"

"Where's the door?"

"I can't stand it, I can't stand it."

"Charlie!"

"*Don't tread on her!*" a woman screamed in an agonized voice.

Then the strangest thing happened; the unbelievable. A man began to sing. He used the microphone, and the loud-speakers carried his voice to every corner. There was something strangely soothing in the sound. There were no words, it was just an air from a popular love song, so enticing, so wheedling, that it seemed to draw panic out of the air.

Someone started to play the piano.

Rickett's voice sounded in Rollison's ear.

"Get moving to that door," something jabbed into Rollison's back. "This is a gun."

Rollison went slowly forward.

.   .   .   .   .

Someone switched on some lights; they were very dim, but they helped.

By the doors there was still a milling crowd, but in the

body of the hall things were quieter. The pianist played the crooner's melody. Uncle Pi, smiling, his shoulders hunched in his red coat, his hands spread out as if he hoped that he could soothe the frightened that way too, swayed from side to side. His smile was the remarkable thing; ineffable.

"Only fireworks," he said, and smiled. "Fools, some people, aren't they? They're trying to scare you—but you can beat them easily. Let's have a song—how about *La Ronde*? We all know the tune of that, don't we?"

He beat time with his hand, the pianist changed the melody.

Redcoats had appeared everywhere; soothing, calming, helping. A few people had fallen, a few were hurt.

Uncle Pi hummed.

Dozens took it up; hundreds; nearly everyone. It rang through the great hall, coming from each of the tiers, the corners, the doorways. These were open. There were no police in sight, they had been carried away by the first crush.

Beck was gone.

The loose-mouthed woman was still there. Ebbutt had gone; so had those of his men whom Rollison would have recognized. Davies was talking to the sergeant, as policemen came hurrying back. Davies looked about, obviously for Rollison, who was near a door—with Rickett poking that thing in his back.

Uncle Pi had won the crowd; he stopped suddenly and began to talk again.

"Of course we've had a bit of trouble at the Camp, it would be silly to deny it, wouldn't it? Some crooks, jewel thieves we believe, had been using it as a place to exchange their loot, but the police had discovered what was happening, and anyhow, didn't the thieves know that the *Toff* was in the Camp?" He laughed, as if delighted; it set people chuckling. "As if anything could go wrong with the Toff around! Not to mention the Redcoats, the Camp Officials, and the police. The crooks won't have a chance! Now, on with the dance!"

"*Da-da-di-da-da-da-da——*"

The people began to dance and sing.

Aird, the Colonel, and Llewellyn appeared on the platform as more light went on, more of the band recovered and took their places.

Davies, near a door, was saying tensely :

"Where's Rollison? Where is he?"

.   .   .   .   .

"All right," Rollison said to Rickett, "don't push."

"Hurry," Rickett muttered. The gun, if it were a gun, was thrust into the small of Rollison's back as they crossed the big hall. They were lost units in a densely packed crowd. "Just keep going."

Outside, the crowd thinned out. It was very dark. Some women were crying, men tried to comfort them. In the poor light, children were still swinging and going on the roundabouts and shrieking their pleasures. More and more people came out of the ballroom, from all the doorways.

"Turn right," growled Rickett.

It might not be a gun.

But if he went, Rollison might see Jolly; and he might be followed by police and Ebbutt's men. Had Ebbutt escaped?

"Get moving!" The thing hurt his ribs.

It was difficult to go much faster.

He had a chance to escape; he had often taken greater risks. He could simply miss a step and back-heel. If it were a gun, the bullet might miss, and if it weren't nothing could go wrong. But if he escaped, what chance was there of finding Jolly?

He could shout : "The airport, the airport!" and police and officials would hear him and carry the message back, but would it help Jolly? Elizabeth? Three missing men?

The crowd had thinned out. The big light over the main diving-platforms was still on, and a few youths were there; the splashes they made came clearly.

"Straight on," Rickett said. "Don't make any mistake."

"Where?"

"By the pool."

Beyond the pool were lawns, flower-beds, and, beyond them, a shrubbery and a wire fence which bordered the road. Cars with their headlights on travelled along the road, and in the shrubberies several men showed up against the glare; they ducked. Anyone following must certainly see them.

"Keep *moving*."

A bullet, and he would be dead. A knife would do, or a silk stocking or a cord tied *tightly*. He was still alive—perhaps only while they were in the Camp. More likely, Beck wanted to find out what he knew.

A car was moving along the road, visible in the glare of the swimming-pool light, and its own sidelights. Men clambered over the wire fence. A second car stood behind the first, engine going.

"Over," Rickett snapped.

Rollison climbed over. He couldn't look round. He had no idea whether they had been followed. He recognized no one. He climbed the wire fence, and then a man standing by one of the cars struck him savagely over the head. The unexpectedness of it was decisive. Rollison didn't dream that it was coming then. He felt as if his skull had been split in two.

He collapsed.

Rickett and the man who had struck Rollison bent down, lifted him and bundled him into the first of the two cars. A third came along. All three cars moved off, headlights blazing.

Rollison was slumped in a corner, with blood oozing from the wound in his head.

CHAPTER XXIII

LAST HOPE?

ROLLISON felt a pain at the back of his head, and a stinging coldness at his face and forehead; and at his neck and chest. He was aware of nothing else—until suddenly it felt as if a hose of ice-cold water had been turned on him. Water shot into his face. He banged his head on something, and pain shrieked through him, but he didn't lose consciousness again.

A man said : "He's awake."

"Make him talk," said another.

It was dark; but Rollison opened his eyes in spite of the pain, and saw the stars; and a gentle crescent moon. He could see the shapes of men, standing round him; and the shape of a building; and the branches of trees.

His arms were tied behind him, to a stake or a small tree.

Cigarettes glowed very red.

Beck said : "Did you tell them where we were going, Rollison?"

Rollison didn't answer. It wasn't because he wouldn't speak; he had that pain at the back of his head, and felt numbed; silly. The question only just made sense.

Beck slapped him across the face, his bony fingers like steel. It was dark, and the only light came from the stars and the cigarettes, but it was possible to imagine that Beck's eyes glowed.

"Did you tell the police?"

Rollison croaked : "No, I didn't."

"It could be a lie," the man said.

There were several people here; four or five. They were all standing beneath the trees. The shed—it couldn't be more than a shed—was quite near. Four cigarettes glowed, and Beck wasn't smoking, so five in all.

"Rollison . . ." Beck said.

"I didn't tell them !"

"Did Jolly?"

"Did he—know?" The question didn't matter, all that mattered was gaining a little time, so that at least he could think. He began to think. They had escaped from the Camp and were at the airfield. Probably they were waiting for an aircraft to come and pick them up.

A car passed along that road, at speed, its headlights blazing. Everyone stood and stared at it; two drew in their breath sharply.

How long had he been here? Was this the airfield? If not, where were they and what were they waiting for?

Davies and Ebbutt knew about the airfield, but was this Butlin's? Perhaps there was another near by.

"How much longer?" a man asked.

"Can't be long." That was Beck. "Only takes two hours each way."

Two hours; almost certainly across the Irish sea.

"We don't want Rollison any more," a man said. It sounded like hard-faced Jake.

"That's right," another agreed.

They were killers; there was the atmosphere of murder about them, from Beck downwards. No one said so, but some were thinking that one more murder would make no difference. For their safety, they depended on getting across the Irish sea. Once over, they would know what to do; they were sure that they could get away. They wouldn't want to take him.

Beck said: "We take him with us and make him talk. We've got to know what he's told the police and what he *thinks* he knows."

"S'right," someone said.

"Beck——" began Rollison.

"Shut up."

"Beck," said Rollison, "is Jolly alive or dead?"

"That's right," Beck said.

It was a sneer. It was meant to keep Rollison in suspense; and it did. It made his heart beat more fiercely and the throbbing pain in his head worse. He knew that he was tied to a tree; that there wouldn't be much chance to free himself.

Another car sped along the road; and then two more, in quick succession. Where *were* the police? And Ebbutt and his men? The road was at least half a mile away, and he could only see it for a short distance; trees hid it for the rest, and also hid this spot from the road. If he shouted, the owls or the bats or the rabbits or the rats might hear him, and the sleeping birds might be disturbed; but that was all.

He began to work at the cords, but the knot was very tight.

Beck said abruptly: *"Listen!"*

Tension sprang into the group. One man dropped a cigarette and trod it out. Rollison sensed that they all stared upwards. There were the stars and the pale moon and wisps of cloud—and there was a slight droning sound.

A man breathed: *"That's it."*

"Won't be long now," Beck said. He moved nearer to Rollison.

The aeroplane was drawing much nearer. Suddenly several beams of light shot out at ground level some way off: landing-lights. Men showed up against the glow. Rollison was facing the landing-field; the aeroplane would come down only a hundred yards or so away from him.

The cord was painfully tight about his wrists.

He said: "Why kidnap Jolly? Why snatch Liz? Why——"

"Shut your trap," Beck growled.

"I can tell you why," another man said, and there was no mistaking his voice.

It was Middleton.

.   .   .   .   .

The other men were watching the aircraft, a dark shape now very near the ground. Middleton fell silent, after that one sentence; and Beck stared at him. Rollison sensed the sudden tension, sensed burning hatred between these two men.

Then: *"I* can tell you," Middleton repeated. "He had to

kidnap Liz because she knew too much—and she knew too much because *I* told her just before he snatched her. And *I* talked because Beck tried to murder me."

"Listen, Dick——" Beck began.

"You're doing the listening, and I've got the drop on you," Middleton said. A gun showed dimly in his hand. "Nice partners, aren't we? Hear that, Rollison, we're *partners*. We smuggle jewels and men out of England to Ireland and then to the li'l ole United States!" His voice thickened, as if he were drunk. He was close enough for the words to reach both Rollison and Beck, although the engine was still roaring and the aircraft was about to land. All the other men were staring at it, some distance from this trio. "I arranged the Camp end of it," Middleton went on. "We needed a spot near the Irish coast where we could hide-out crooks who'd made things too hot for them over here. Didn't we, Beck? We——"

"Listen, Dick——" Beck began.

"Shut up!" Middleton said viciously, "or I'll shoot your guts out."

The aeroplane had landed and was running along the landing-strip. The very ground seemed to tremble.

"What better place than the Camp?" Middleton asked shrilly. "Go on, tell me that, Rollison—can *you* think of one? We booked single chalets for imaginary people, and when we wanted to hide a wanted man, he came and took over a reserved chalet. It was fool-proof. The only difficulty was in getting them up in the air. They took the free transport to the airfield with other Campers, didn't they Beck? Every now and again we run a charter service to Ireland, so we took them across. No trouble at all, it was a brilliant idea. We had to bribe some of the ground staff and the pilot, and fix airfield jobs for Beck's men. It was easy—except for one thing. Liz got suspicious about something she heard Beck and Clark say on their first visit. She told Campion, the first missing Redcoat. He tried to find out what it was all about, and we had to kidnap him. He took a ride in the bus to the airfield and didn't come back.

"Liz told me she was worried.

"I convinced her there was nothing to worry about," Middleton went on hoarsely. "I said that I'd do all the necessary. *And* I did! Campion had talked to the other missing Redcoats—we snatched them the same way. They just stepped into the free transport to the airfield and were knocked out among the trees. Easy! Then whenever we had to send a man to Ireland we took a prisoner over, too. We packed their bags and tried to make it all look voluntary, but Aird was worried, and he told the Colonel, and that brought *you*, Mr. Ruddy Toff."

"Listen, Dick, you've got——" Beck began.

The engine of the aircraft stopped, abruptly. Silence seemed to fill the world. There was hardly a sound, until the men ahead started to run towards the aircraft, and someone called :

"Come on, Cy."

"You're not going anywhere, and I'll tell you why," said Middleton, hoarsely. "Liz began to help Rollison. She knew a bit and guessed some more—she guessed that I'd done nothing about looking for the others, and it made her think I might be mixed up in it. But she was in love with me. Beck knew what she might do, he wanted to snatch her and kill her, but I wouldn't let it happen. *I wouldn't*! I was sure I could keep Liz quiet. But Beck got scared. Do you know what, Rollison, he didn't trust me any longer. He nearly murdered me. Then he snatched Liz. He thought I would be too scared to talk, and he was right—but I wasn't too scared to come and get my own back. He tried to kill me, but I'm going to do more than try—I'm going to kill him."

Rollison heard a stealthy sound before Middleton guessed that anyone else was there. Rollison began to call a warning, but was too late. A man who had crept behind Middleton smashed a weapon on to the back of his head; Middleton went down, making a choking sound.

"Cy, we've got to hurry, we can't lose any time." It was Rickett. "Cars are coming along without light, they aren't so far away. I reckon the police are in them. We've got to kill Rollison——"

The darkness was slashed by bright lights—headlamps and torches, a few hundred yards away. The engine of the aircraft started up again. Most of the men were already near it, clambering in.

". . . and kill Middleton, we've got to——"

"Okay," Beck said. "It's a pleasure."

In the light, dim just here, he took out a gun.

If this fired bullets, it meant death. Rollison, helpless, rigid against the tree, could only wait for split seconds that brought agony.

Beck bent over Middleton, and Rollison heard the hiss of the gas pistol. Had he saved his own life, when emptying those phials?

Beck turned on him and squeezed the trigger. Cool *air* streamed into Rollison's face. The gas phials were empty of gas.

If Beck should guess——

Rollison screamed and screwed up his face and began to choke. Satisfied, Beck and Rickett turned away and raced towards the aircraft. Police were still a hundred yards away.

Beck looked a giant scarecrow, Rickett massive and brutish, as they ran.

Men crashed through the undergrowth near Rollison, and a man called out:

"Mr. Rollison—Mr. *Ar!*" That was Ebbutt.

It was safe to answer . . .

But Beck and Rickett and the rest of the gang were in the aircraft, the police couldn't stop them from taking off.

Ebbutt rushed up.

Davies called out.

The aircraft, its engine roaring, moved along the runway and then soared into the air.

CHAPTER XXIV

FINALE

THERE was another sound near Rollison as Ebbutt cut his bonds, and the police made a futile rush towards the air-craft.

A man gave a choking laugh.

"Wot——" began Ebbutt.

"Watch him!" Rollison exclaimed. "That's Middleton, and he's armed."

"Oh, *is* 'e?" Ebbutt moved swiftly, bent over Middleton, and took his gun. "Soon put that right." He lugged Middleton to his feet, and stood him against a tree, not very gently.

Middleton still laughed in a queer, unnatural way; a choking laugh. It was as if madness had suddenly taken possession of him. In the different beams of light, all bright, his lips were drawn back.

Men stood and watched the aircraft as it blotted out the stars where it passed.

Others came towards Middleton; Aird, Davies, Llewellyn, and Uncle Pi. There were a lot of police and a lot of Redcoats; nearly everyone carried a torch.

"What's got into Middleton, now?" Davies asked. "What's so funny?"

"Funny," Middleton gasped. "Funny!" He didn't look sane. "Funny," he choked, and then he screamed: "*Look, look, look!*"

The starlit sky was split by a yellowish orange flame; a great roar came back to them; then they saw fire in the air, and knew exactly what had happened.

Pieces of the burning aircraft fell to the ground and split into tiny fragments and spread in a great area. A piece of wreckage crashed and shook the ground.

"Did he *know*?" breathed Davies.

"Of course he knew," Rollison said, in a voice which he

hardly recognized as his own. His head was an aching ball, he didn't know how to keep his eyes open. Jolly—Liz—where were they? *Where?* "He sent them to crash, meant to sit pretty himself. That's why he wouldn't travel with them. Grab him!"

Middleton was still laughing, as if his mind had been turned, when the police handcuffed him.

"I did it!" he screeched. "I gave a time bomb to Rickett, just a little thing, he thought it was a jewel-case. Perfect timing, wasn't it, perfect——"

He broke off into laughter again, then slumped forward, unconscious from loss of blood.

They went back across the fields towards the car, Rollison carried in a "chair" made by Ebbutt and another East Ender. Middleton was between two police-sergeants; he was no longer giggling; but for support he would have fallen.

Davies talked; explaining.

One of Bill Ebbutt's men had climbed to the top of a water tower, to watch the cars as they had driven off. He had been able to tell the police that the cars had turned off the road at a certain spot, and Camp officials had placed it beyond doubt as the airfield.

Cars with police, Redcoats, and officials had driven past the approach to the airfield, then doubled back, using side-lights and able to coast because the road led downhill. They had walked across fields and infiltrated into the woods. Others had approached across country, and had been on the other side of the road near the airfield gates. Over fifty men had been in that final raid, and they had waited until the aeroplane landed, to make a sudden swoop.

They had waited too long.

Only Middleton could tell them the whole story, and say where the prisoners were.

They reached the road, with Davies still talking.

There had been one other capture: Rickett's wife.

Ebbutt helped Rollison into a car.

Middleton began to laugh again. He was stupid with it. The law would probably say that he was guilty but insane.

On his unhinged mind depended the lives of Jolly, Elizabeth, and three Redcoats.

At the Camp Rollison was taken to the Sick Bay and his wound dressed. He wasn't present when Davies first questioned Middleton.

Sometimes Middleton grinned, sometimes he giggled, sometimes he was silent; he did not give a single intelligible answer. A doctor stopped the questioning.

"You'll never get any sense out of him while he's like this, and I can't allow any more. He's a hospital case."

Rollison learned all this when he was up, and went to Aird's office. Aird, the Colonel, Llewellyn, and Davies were there, with the grey-haired woman and Uncle Pi, whose eyes seemed deeply shadowed.

The grey-haired woman said: "Mr. Rollison, isn't there anything you can suggest?"

Rollison said: "Yes. Where's Beck's wife?"

"She doesn't know a thing about where they usually go," Davies declared. "I've talked to her until I'm blue in the face. She doesn't know Beck's dead yet, though. She says that he didn't confide in her much. She knew something was happening here and that men and jewels were smuggled out of the Camp by the aircraft, but that's all."

"Will this help *Jolly*?" the grey-haired woman asked, and there was anguish in her voice.

Uncle Pi said hurtfully: "I don't think it will help anyone."

Rollison barked: "It's time you talked, Wray. Try explaining why you were in Middleton's chalet when he was nearly killed. Why you went to Liz's afterwards? Why——"

Uncle Pi said steadily: "I went to see if Liz was in Middleton's chalet. I stood listening in the doorway for some time—I didn't go in."

"Why listen? Why eavesdrop?"

"I thought Middleton was no good and wanted Liz to find out by herself. If they'd been in there together, I'd have got her away, somehow. Later I went to her chalet to see if I could find out where she'd gone."

"It could even be true," Rollison growled. "But we've got to know all we can before talking to Rosa Beck. What did Rosa know, Davies?"

"Beck, Clark, and Middleton have been bringing stolen jewels and flying them to American, Canadian, and Continental buyers in Ireland. They sold the stuff for dollars or other hard currency—never for sterling. There was a steady traffic in men, too—all crooks on the Yard's wanted list. Beck fixed forged passports and visas. They hoped to get two more men away, at least—men now at the Camp. Mrs. Beck's named them."

No one else spoke; but Uncle Pi glanced impatiently at the door.

"Elizabeth Cherrell overheard some planning, and . . ." Davies told Rollison what he already knew, then added grimly : "That's all Mrs. Beck admits to knowing—except that she was a victim of a faked attack, with the idea of pretending to be scared into talking to you, so that she could put us on the wrong track about the Caves at Harlech. You saw through that man, didn't you?"

"I didn't see far enough," Rollison growled. "When can we tackle Middleton again?"

Davies said regretfully : "He's not right in the head, Mr. Rollison. We cannot rely on him for any common sense, and we cannot overdo it."

That was true, and had to be faced.

"I'd make Mrs. Beck talk if I had to strangle her——" Uncle Pi began hoarsely.

"Let me do the strangling," said Rollison. "Where is she?"

"Still in the hospital," Davies told him.

.   .   .   .   .

Rosa Beck's hair looked like beaten brass. Her eyes were heavy. She looked exhausted, and there was no interest in her expression when Rollison came in. Just outside the door were Davies and Aird; by the open window, two others, including Uncle Pi. But in this little room Rollison and the woman appeared to be alone.

Rollison pulled up a chair.

"Better?" he asked.

"I've nothing to say to you—nothing at all."

"Think again," Rollison said softly. "And forget all your hopes, Rosa. Cy's dead."

That shook her. She looked at him sharply, in sudden fear.

"That's a lie!"

"He's dead. Middleton blew up the aeroplane. Cy was making his last journey in it. Middleton kept away." He paused. She believed him—and what mattered was that she should believe the lie now on his lips: "Middleton's on his way to the hide-out. He wants to pick up the cash that's there, take Liz Cherrell, and get away. Is that your idea of a happy ending : Cy dead, Middleton sitting pretty?"

"It's a lie," Rosa gasped again.

"All right," Rollison said, very slowly. "You think it's a lie, but I know it's true. I saw the aeroplane blow up. I know how you felt about Cy. I know that you were one of the few who weren't afraid of him. I know how cleverly you tried to fool me. I pretended to believe you, but was quite sure they weren't in any cave. Now listen. It isn't your fault that Cy's dead. It will be your fault if Middleton gets away with this. Where's the hide-out? I want to be there, waiting for him."

Her eyes had the burning intensity that had once been Cy Beck's.

"Cy's—*dead,*" she breathed. "You mean it!"

"I'm sorry, Rosa."

"Go and get Middleton!" she screamed. "Catch him, hang him. He's at . . ."

.   .   .

Ten hours later, Rollison and Uncle Pi and a grey-haired woman, whom Rollison now knew to be Lilian Small, were together in a car when the Eire police raided a small house not far from the Ulster border.

There was a rough landing-strip near by; a so-called

"amateur" aero club; three guards who were taken completely by surprise; two men wanted for murder by Scotland Yard; and the prisoners—*alive*.

Jolly was shaken but unhurt. When he saw Lilian Small, his eyes lit up.

Elizabeth was frightened, bruised, but still so very beautiful; when Uncle Pi went towards her, she saw something in his eyes which told her great truths. He must have been satisfied by all that he saw in hers.

There were also two thin, emaciated men, who still wore their red coats, and one who would soon have been as bad.

There was a good hoard of stolen jewels; of dollars; and the names of the crooks still waiting at the Camp to be smuggled abroad—as well as a list of all who had been taken out of the country and information which would help the police to trace them and bring them back.

.   .   .   .

More facts soon came out.

How Elizabeth, once in love with Middleton and ever loyal, had gradually lost her faith in him; but he had fought to save her from Beck, who would have been ruthless. There had been that much good in Middleton.

How the missing Redcoats had left in the airfield wagon, been hailed when it was near the airfield, lured among the trees, attacked, and sent to Ireland with the next smuggler-'plane. Beck and the gang had not wanted to kill for the sake of it—had planned to finish the game and go to the States, leaving the men alive.

How Beck had planted the jewels in Elizabeth's chalet, while planning her capture, hoping to make the police think she had run away for fear of being found out. Beck had been prepared to do anything to gain precious time.

How Jolly had been waylaid, simply to give Beck a stranglehold on Rollison.

How Susan Dell had been a nervous wreck, dangerous to Beck and the gang; and been murdered. Clark, in love with her, had threatened trouble and been killed swiftly.

How Middleton had invented a wife he had to visit when he had to get away from the Camp; and, falling in love with Elizabeth, found his "wife" a liability, but talked of her so that he could win general sympathy—especially Elizabeth's. And how the desire to break away from Beck and live a normal life had become an obsession, turning his mind because he feared Beck so.

So he had twisted and turned, trying to discredit Rollison, fearful of what Elizabeth or Rollison might discover, fearful of Beck, but, even after Beck had nearly killed him, unable to unmask the man.

And how Uncle Pi had persuaded Aird to talk to the Colonel, and so begin the Toff's investigation—because Uncle Pi had believed that Elizabeth was in danger from a Middleton who wasn't quite sane.

.   .   .   .

There was a great concourse of people at the gates of the Camp. Only the toddlers remained at the swimming-baths. Most of the halls and games rooms, the playing-fields, the milk bars, and the licensed bars were also deserted. The throng was crowding to see Rollison's car as he drove with Jolly by his side.

The Colonel and Aird had already said good-bye, and given their thanks.

Ebbutt and his men had gone home.

Uncle Pi was with Elizabeth, for once neglecting the Camp's children; and Elizabeth was well and much less troubled.

The three rescued Redcoats were in hospital.

The flags bordering the Camp fluttered gaily in a stiffish breeze which stirred the waters of the pools and the leaves of the trees and bushes, but the sun shone brightly, and the water and the distant sea were blue. The mountains were capped with purple haze, lending them beauty.

The crowd was waving, laughing, cheering.

The gate-keepers waved.

Just outside, making a kind of guard of honour, were a

hundred Redcoats, men and girls, laughing, waving. And then, as they went out of the gates, the Camp bands struck up a triumphal march.

At last, they were past all this and on the open road.

"Jolly," said Rollison, "you've got to admit that they do things in style."

"I couldn't agree with you more, sir," said Jolly. "As you are well aware, I was extremely dubious about the wisdom of accepting the commission; and having accepted it, doubtful whether we should find that we could—ah—endure the atmosphere."

Rollison kept a straight face.

"But we survived."

"We did indeed," said Jolly. "In fact, I freely admit that I would willingly have stayed longer, if only because I so greatly enjoyed the company of Mrs. Small, who was a *great* help in all my inquiries. She has been at the Camps for so long that everyone knew her and no one was surprised that she asked questions. But for her I am doubtful whether we would have discovered as much as we did in the short time at our disposal," went on Jolly, pretending to be bland but speaking rather more quickly than usual; as if not quite sure of himself. "I understand that she had decided that this will be her last season at the Camps, she is to spend all her time at the organization's London Headquarters. They are not so very far removed from Gresham Terrace," Jolly added; and rested, glancing sharply at Rollison.

"Well, well!" marvelled Rollison. "How very convenient! We owe her so much that it would be most inconsiderate not to take every opportunity to express our gratitude, wouldn't it? Of course," he added solemnly, "you could show it in other ways. I suppose your room at the flat *could* be turned into marriage quarters, if——"

"I think, if I may say so, sir," murmured Jolly, "that we are being a little previous in considering that. There are other matters worth attention, too. In addition to the original fee, there is to be a substantial bonus. The insurance companies will pay you a recovery commission for the jewels found in Ireland. A *most* satisfactory ending, sir, on the whole."

He was relaxed; smiling.

Long before they reached Bala, for they chose to go home that way, he was humming the light air from *La Ronde*.